T0129396

Light and Color
Inside or Outside

JOHN S. MUNDAY

ARCHWAY PUBLISHING

Archway Publishing books may be ordered
through booksellers or by contacting:

Archway Publishing
1663 Liberty Drive
Bloomington, IN 47403
www.archwaypublishing.com
1 (888) 242-5904

ISBN: 978-1-4808-7422-0 (sc)
ISBN: 978-1-4808-7421-3 (e)

Library of Congress Control Number: 2019900739

Print information available on the last page.

Archway Publishing rev. date: 02/01/2019

Acknowledgments

Many years ago, my wife, Fran Wohlenhaus-Munday, and I lived in a town house in Ocean City, Maryland. It had many delights, including a pair of pigeons that roosted on the top level of our deck. The pigeon I liked best I named Rembrandt because of its vivid color. Fran named the other pigeon Monet because of its delightfully soft colors, which reminded her of impressionist art. In addition to books showing Monet's art, Fran has collected prints by Monet that delight us both. Fran walked the long journey with me in my writing this novel. Thank you, my lovely muse.

He Would Be Lucky

Since he would be going to Giverny tomorrow to work in Claude Monet's gardens, Jean Forgeron quickly packed a bag with clothes to take. He then went out to the Café de la Nouvelle Athénes at 11 Grande rue des Batignolles, passing other pedestrians who seemed to be window-shopping as he walked the streets. The café held special memories for him because Jean had met Claude Monet there more than two years ago, on his first visit to the café. When he'd come into the café, he'd seen a group of artists at a set of tables, talking about art in its many forms—plus drinking, of course—with some of them looking for ladies, either to have the women model for them or for other purposes. They had pulled three of the marble-topped tables together to tighten the group of artists. Jean had sat alone at a table near the artists, not looking at the people sitting at the tables. He'd ordered a glass of wine and relaxed. The smell of smoke and alcohol pleased Jean. Edgar Degas, whom Jean had taken a few lessons from, had come over to him. "Jean, come on over to our table."

"Yes, sir!" Jean had gone to the vacant chair next to Degas, smiling at the group. He'd taken a deep breath as he met Camille Pissarro and several others. He'd forgotten them when Claude Monet stood up and warmly greeted him with a big smile. He also had waved to the waitress for another drink.

Degas had spoken up. "Jean has shown much promise as an artist."

Monet had asked, "What has this young wannabe done to support that opinion?"

"I have given Jean lessons, and he learned quickly what I taught him. Also, Jean's strokes are similar to Monet's paintings."

Monet had laughed and said, "No one has strokes like I do, and if you don't know that, you should give up art." Degas had replied that he would give up art if Monet did.

To defuse what he saw as too much tension, which he later understood to be typical of their exchanges, Jean had interrupted them to ask Monet about his gardens. Monet had asked Jean why he wanted to know about his gardens, and Jean had told him he loved gardens. They'd talked for a moment about when poppies should be planted and when they might bloom. Jean had told Monet, "More poppies come back every spring, and I love the bright red color," which had turned out to be just enough knowledge to survive the questioning.

Monet had said, "Jean, you could work in my gardens and maybe even learn why my strokes are only mine."

A week later, Jean had gone to Giverny, where he'd worked as a gardener for two years, except for occasional trips back to his studio in Montmartre. Back home, Jean also found occasional models who gave him what he needed as an artist.

That evening, after two glasses of pinot noir, Jean saw a lovely lady sitting alone, and he left the table to talk with her. As he stood up, Degas asked him what he would do if she were married. Jean rubbed his hands together as a first reply and then said, "Edgar, I've learned that most men see women as single or married. I see them as faithful or available."

At the lady's table, Jean introduced himself as Jean Forgeron, an artist with a studio in Montmartre. Almost immediately, she said she would agree to model for him if he would pay her forty francs.

"You are very attractive, but your price far exceeds what I would pay." Jean put both of his hands in his pants pockets.

She replied that she would model for him, and then they could talk price. Jean didn't feel right about her proposition, if that was what she intended. He had hoped to be lucky that evening but not in that way. After waving to her, Jean went back to his table and smiled as the others teased him. Then one artist said that the woman might not have been a good model, but nevertheless, she sure could respond to an attempt at intimacy. Others laughed in agreement.

"Are you speaking from experience?" Jean asked. "Is she part of the initiation routine here?" Someone patted Jean on the shoulder for that remark. Jean ordered another glass of wine.

For Each of Their Opinions

At the Café de la Nouvelle Athénes that evening, some of his artist friends were laughing about two ladies who had been at the café before Jean got there. Pissarro said, "Neither lady would join this table of artists. They walked past the table to their own, as far from the artists as they could get and still be inside the café."

"Are they old ladies?" Jean asked.

"I went over to them," Degas said, "because I had previously given them one short lesson, and I hope to become their art instructor. I said, 'Ladies, I don't know if you have any talent as artists, but I will be honored to instruct you. I'm well known as an artist and as an instructor.' Then I told them I enjoy teaching Mary Cassatt to be an artist."

They both affirmed that Ms. Cassatt already had succeeded as an artist. Degas said he'd offered to introduce them to Ms. Cassatt, who was from near Philadelphia. When he'd gotten back to the other artists, he'd shown them that the ladies had written their names and hometowns on a napkin.

"Luisa Magdalena Slagle will be on the train to Giverny

tomorrow. The napkin says she is from America, having been raised in Bryn Mawr, Pennsylvania, a wealthy suburb west of Philadelphia," Degas told Jean. "She is going to Giverny to explore Monet's painting methods and techniques at his suggestion."

Jean smiled at the thought that maybe he would hear Monet say something he could use in his own art. Monet always talked about painting and often about technique. Degas had told her that in light of Monet's experience, she would be better off if she didn't bring her artwork"

Emille Martha Tveger was also from a Philadelphia suburb, one a bit southwest of the city, Drexel Hill, which had some wealthy residences. "The two ladies just recently met when they both went to an art show in Montmartre. They recognized each other's Philadelphia-style dresses, which are fluid, soft silhouettes with a high neckline. They both wore a large hat and had short hair." That they were both going to visit Monet was a coincidence one of the ladies called good fortune and the other called a sign.

Because they'd left before Jean got to the café, Degas gave him the napkin when he learned that Jean too planned to go to Giverny tomorrow. "Jean, I can assure you that they are both lovely ladies but too reserved to sit with people who have not been introduced to them. American culture won't allow proper ladies to dance with anyone they have not been properly introduced to as well."

"I know the type," Jean said. "They are cultured but also proper. They live their code. I would enjoy meeting them. I'm hoping somehow to be introduced."

It surprised Jean that Degas had their full names and hometowns.

Degas said, "It's what I did with you, Jean. Remember? I get that information from all of my students. These ladies are likely to be my students. I told them about Mary Cassatt and my artwork with her. The two ladies wanted to meet her."

Based on Edgar's enthusiasm for the two ladies, Jean decided to bring some of his artwork along so he could ask for their opinions.

He didn't need or want their opinions but thought it might open the door to one or the other. He wished he had gotten to the café in time to see them. *But now,* he thought, *they won't know I have their names and approval from Degas.*

Suddenly, several of the artists at the table started to shout at the man who'd just come into the café: Émile Zola, a novelist well known to those at the table. Jean stood to greet him. Zola casually waved to Jean and took a seat across the table from him.

Degas also waved to Zola and then said, "Congratulations, Émile, on your literary successes." For everyone's benefit, he went on to say, "We are mostly artists, and Émile joins us from time to time to share his political views, most of which we agree with. What are you working on now?"

"Edgar, you all agree with me more than you agree with each other."

Most of the artists voiced approval of what Zola had said about them. Some even laughed.

The conversation turned to art finally, including how their art had helped Émile Zola construct his newest novels. "I'm not writing about art directly. It's the creativity that your paintings give me that drives me to create words on a page. The novel I'm working on now—and it is almost finished—is based on my travel to Lourdes to see the miracles being made—if you believe that the miracles are real. I don't. I saw only people using hope to have a true medical healing." Zola went on to say religion was false as well as a waste of time for those who participated in its services.

Jean excused himself, mentioning the early train to Giverny the next morning. He had been raised Catholic, as most French children were, and had even been an altar boy. An image of himself in a solid red outfit and red cap came to mind. He felt unsure about his faith now in his adult life, but his response to an attack on the miracles at Lourdes helped him realize he still believed, though he also realized he didn't know what he believed.

It's Good Enough for Us

Jean stopped walking away from the café when he thought he had gained enough distance from it to relax. He looked up at the sky, pounding his right fist into his left hand. He heard someone call his name and started walking away; then he realized the call had come from in front of him, not from the café.

Paul Cézanne came up to Jean and took his hand to greet him. "Jean, how are you? Is the group ended? How are you?"

"I'm fine, Paul—sort of. The group is still there. Zola is telling them about his new book. About Lourdes. About how God doesn't make miracles happen." He looked around for a place to sit. "You know him from way back. Is he like that?"

"Émile Zola is like that. He is—well, I'll have to think of the word, but Émile is a lot of things at one time. Let's go around this corner. There's a place down there." Cézanne took Jean by the arm and led him to a café that was part of a hotel not known for progressive gatherings. Other artists would not have thought of that café.

Jean continued to look up at the sky as they sat at a table outside the café. Cézanne watched him and then spoke as he too looked up. "Are you looking for God up there? By the way, I became a Catholic a little over a year ago. I find comfort in just sitting alone in church with nothing happening, except God and I are together. And I haven't yet found a priest I can engage in conversation with."

"Do you go to Mass? My parents raised me as a Catholic, and I enjoyed hearing the scripture readings. My father had a Bible from England, which we weren't supposed to read. But I did." Jean sat back, smiled, and took a sip of the wine he had ordered. "This is good wine, but I don't hide in it like some artists do. Anyway, what is it that has Zola going on against Lourdes?"

"Émile is part of that group of intellectuals who talk about what is called French naturalism. They are fighting the Catholics specifically and all religions as well. They want nature to be in charge. Émile and I were friends from childhood until he published a fictionalized depiction of me as part of the bohemian life of painters in his novel *The Masterpiece* in 1886. It didn't come close to describing me, but people thought I lived that ridiculous way. Anyway, how are you and Monet doing?"

"Fine. I'm going to Giverny tomorrow to start work again as his gardener. You did some work with Claude too, didn't you?"

"Some in the 1870s. He did brighten my color palette. We're still friends. I prefer to paint indoors, but I also do a lot of *en plein air* of houses and landscapes. Most of my paintings are small, like a still life with fruit or books. You know."

"Yes, I do, and he says nice things about you. But to stay on my subject, I don't know why Zola upset me so. Should I worry about it, Paul?"

"Does it affect your faith?"

"Ha. You answered my question with a question, the answer to which answers my question. When I went to Mass as a young man, one time, a priest said rabbis taught that way. And he said the disciples called Jesus a rabbi, or teacher. The Good Samaritan story shows Jesus hearing a question and answering with a question. And since it doesn't affect my faith, that answers my question, and I won't worry about what Zola is saying."

As they talked, Cézanne mentioned that he not only had become a Catholic but also had another joy in his life. "Hortense Figuet and I were married in 1886 after being together for a while. We have a good life together."

Eventually, the subject turned to what other artists were doing. When Pissarro walked past the café, not looking to see if anyone sat inside, Jean insisted Cézanne stay quiet, saying, "Our group doesn't need to know I felt upset with what Zola said."

Almost as an afterthought, Cézanne asked Jean if he knew the name of the pope.

"I'm not sure. Pope Pius IX served as pope when I grew up. But I don't know."

"Pius IX lasted a long time as pope, but Pope Leo III took office and installed on February 20, 1878. Zola wants to talk with the pope."

That topic of conversation didn't go any further, as Jean didn't know what to say.

After a while, Jean declined another glass of wine, telling Cézanne he needed to get up early and already had had two glasses in the café. "What are you working on now?"

"I've started a series of paintings of Provençal peasants playing cards. I'm having a lot of fun. I have four of them: one standing between their table and a wall and the other three sitting at the table, looking at the cards in their hands. All four have hats, coats, and vests. They wouldn't expose their shirts when I asked them to do so. Behind them, on the wall, is a row of smoking pipes in a bracket."

Jean said he could see the painting in his mind. "Did any of them use one of those pipes to smoke?"

Jean and Cézanne both stood. Cézanne paid the tab and walked off to the café to see the other artists. Jean went home to get some rest before he traveled in the morning.

If He Followed Them

The next morning, Jean got to the Saint-Lazare station before the train arrived. After getting his ticket, he sat on a bench with his sketchbook in his hands, though he didn't see anything he wanted to sketch. A black engine pulled into the station, pouring out steam, as the engineer peered out the side. The train stopped at the raised platform so riders could get on either of the two passenger cars.

Two women Jean assumed were Luisa Magdalena Slagle and Emille Martha Tveger showed up, bought their tickets, and went to board the back car. Jean noted the Philadelphia-style dresses and concluded they were whom he wanted to meet. He saw each of them look at him before climbing the steps to get in the car. Maybe they noticed him because of his open sketchbook. He couldn't see if either of the ladies smiled. He got up and climbed the same stairs to get on the train.

As he came into the back car, he saw one of them following the other, using the doors between the cars to enter the other car. He thought if he followed them, they surely would know he was interested in them, so he sat down by a window and relaxed. Jean knew the ladies were interested in art, and he was looking to Monet to use him in his interactions with them. Jean felt his shirt pocket to remind himself he had Monet's letter to show them. Philadelphia ladies would want a proper introduction or an opportunity to learn what they wanted to know from him. He had a plan for both options. He told himself it was like either finding a gate to a fence or finding a place to climb over it.

∞

The two women found seats they liked. Emille said, "You get the window going, Luisa, and I'll get it on the way back."

"Thanks. That will work," Luisa replied.

They both settled into their seats, rearranging their skirts and small bags. Emille said the seat felt too narrow, and she had to be careful not to let her skirt bend to show her ankles. Earlier that morning, they'd decided to bring what they needed to stay overnight. They also had brought several of their drawings. Hopefully Monet would ask to see them, though Degas had told them not to show them to Monet or even bring them to Giverny. Back in Philadelphia, their instructors always wanted to see their work and gave suggestions for improving the art. Emille wondered to herself if Paris and Philadelphia not only looked different but also were different.

Soon the train started to move, lurching at first and then settling into a bit of a rocky ride. The views of the French countryside amazed them both but did not keep them from talking. Luisa took out her drawings, telling Emille that they weren't bad, and she hoped Mr. Monet would give her some good advice.

Emille looked at the drawings and patted Luisa's shoulder. "Those are good drawings—better than mine, which means I will get more help from Mr. Monet." They both laughed and looked at each other. They continued to watch the scenery and let their minds absorb being in France.

Luisa commented that the French countryside looked a lot different from Paris. Emille nodded in agreement, saying, "It's like going west from Philadelphia. All country until you get to Pittsburgh. My father says the land between Philadelphia and Pittsburgh is just more of West Virginia."

Their train made good time and soon pulled into the station at Vernon.

If He Doesn't Make It with the Ladies

Jean leaned back to relax after putting his bag and hat on the seat next to him so he would be alone. He considered it important that he enjoy the scenic countryside as the train rolled along at a good pace. He put his sketchbook back into his pack when he decided the train's speed prevented him from sketching a scene. Jean thought about what Zola had said the night before about miracles. He had never been to Lourdes but had heard many people rave about the miracles. He decided Zola lived in another world, and he put the conversation out of his mind. Jean had his own religious issues and didn't need to have Zola—or anyone else, for that matter—preach to him. In his youth, he had been told that his faith remained between himself and God. He didn't remember who had told him that, but several priests had tried to make him listen to them, not to God.

Jean noticed a young man talking to one of the other passengers in the car. He wore casual clothes, as if he worked as a gardener of the kind Monet would hire. His cotton jacket would protect him from thorns and other plants. When he went to Jean, the man said, "Are you going to Giverny?"

"Who says I am?" Jean replied.

The man's accent confirmed Jean's suspicion that he too was French. Jean also noticed that the young man had a pack, as Jean did. Was he an artist?

"You look like one who would, or should, go to the gardens."

Jean wore white pants, a blue shirt under a plaid vest, and a dark jacket that would protect him in the gardens.

"Why do you care?" Jean didn't like for people to pry into his life, even though so far, prying could be resisted.

The young man stood next to Jean's seat, looking intently at him. "I'm learning to be an artist. If you are an artist and you know Monet, maybe you'll introduce me to him."

"Okay. Yes, I am going to Mr. Monet's gardens. And that is enough about me."

"Mr. Monet? Why not Monet or Claude?" He smiled.

"I have always shown respect for Mr. Monet. I don't know you and can't possibly introduce you to Mr. Monet because he respects me, and I don't want to disappoint him. Find someone else. I am using this time on the train for my own reasons."

The man did not walk away. "Are you an artist? Are you a gardener?"

"Yes."

"Which one?"

"Both. Now, leave me so I can enjoy the ride while it lasts."

The man frowned and then wandered toward the other passenger car.

Jean went back to his thoughts and memories of working as a gardener in 1890 and 1891, after Mr. Monet had bought the house and land for his gardens. Jean worked as one of his gardeners and had helped build the greenhouse and studio. Monet let him come into the studio, with its skylights, to see his paintings. He'd learned quite a bit about Monet's style of art, surviving some difficult lessons. Jean had learned that Monet taught what he believed was right and had no interest in opposite points of view. He did not tolerate ignorance of the issue at hand.

As the train slowed for the station in Vernon, Jean thought about the new land Monet had purchased. He had heard it had a water meadow. *Well,* he thought, *if I don't make it with the ladies, at least I'll have the fun of hearing what plans the artist has for his gardens.* He also felt he should talk further to the young man. Jean regretted not asking him if he painted or gardened. Though the man had gone to the other passenger car after talking with Jean, Jean expected to be approached again by the young man when they got to Giverny. Jean put his hands together as if praying, bringing them up to his chin. He wanted to think about what he would say to Monet, if anything at all.

One Bale at Different
Times of the Day

J ean took his time in getting off the train when it arrived in Vernon, in part because he felt relaxed and in part so he wouldn't look as if he had a serious interest in the ladies. He expected them to ride the shuttle to the Giverny station and hoped he could get a seat that would allow him to talk with them. At the least, he would have an opportunity to see them close up, so he could consider their facial features as an artist.

As he stepped down from the car, the young artist wannabe came over to Jean. "Sir, I apologize for interrupting your time on the train. You're an artist and have a creative mind. I know now I should have left you alone so you could think."

"That's fine," Jean said. "My name is Jean Forgeron." He saw that the ladies were getting on the shuttle, so he headed that way. "Are you an artist? Or a gardener? Or both?"

"I want to be an artist. My name is Pierre Stéphane. Please call me Pierre. I have started lessons and hope to get some help from, um, Mr. Monet."

"Okay, Pierre, let's get on the shuttle."

"Oh no, I'm walking. I'm short of money. It's not that far, is it?"

He looked at Jean as if he wanted Jean to buy his ticket. *No way,*

Jean thought. He'd interfere with Jean's chance to talk with the ladies. "Go for it. I'll talk with you when I get a chance at Giverny."

Jean got on the shuttle, which had seats facing forward and backward. The ladies insisted on facing the direction of travel. He sat facing backward on the seat in front of them. He waved to Pierre and looked out the window as the shuttle started to move.

Jean waited until they'd left the station, and then he spoke to the ladies, telling them his name and adding that he was both an artist and a gardener. He hoped that would impress them. He mentioned that two of his paintings hung in the Café de la Nouvelle Athénes and added that they might enjoy the art if they ever went to the café. They didn't reply, so he then told them of his two years there in Giverny, working for Mr. Monet as a gardener. He showed them the letter in which Monet had invited him to work as a gardener again. He added that they should call him Jean.

One of the women spoke. "My name is Luisa Magdalena Slagle. I am from a suburb of Philadelphia and am learning about art. I am an artist, I hope. It is a pleasure to meet you, Mr. Forgeron. You know Mr. Monet quite well, I assume." She shifted in her seat. "Please call me Luisa."

Before Jean could reply, the other woman spoke. "My name is Emille Martha Tveger, and please call me Emille. Would you tell us a bit about Mr. Monet? Do you, um, think he might look at our artwork? Would he help us?"

The question gave him a dilemma. If he told them the truth, not even knowing what quality of artwork they had made, they would be angry with him. They wouldn't believe that Monet disliked all art by others. If he lied, they would find out for themselves how Monet felt about the art of others, and they would be angry with him. Then Jean remembered what Degas had said about their art and Monet. "Did your instructor tell you what to do when you got to Giverny? In fact, who is your art instructor?"

Emille laughed and said, "Degas warned us not to show our art."

"Even if he asks to see it," Luisa said. They looked at each other with a smile.

"You found the right answer, Mr. Forgeron," Emille said.

Luisa added, "Yes, you did, Jean."

He felt as though the conversation would serve as his introduction to them.

After that, the three of them were silent as they rode along. He kept looking out the window at the farm fields they passed. He tried to see if either lady took an opportunity to look at him, but neither did. Instead, they sneaked looks only at each other. He wondered how long they had known each other. Then he excitedly pointed to a stack of hay bales. "Look! There are hay bales like the ones Mr. Monet painted. Can you see how the light affects the color?"

The ladies took turns looking out the window.

"Are those the ones Monet painted?" Luisa asked. "In the series, they all look so different, even though I think he painted just one bale at different times of day."

"One bale at different times of the day. Be sure to ask to see any of the series he still has in his studio."

"It sounds like Mr. Forgeron has seen the series, Luisa," Emille said. Both ladies continued to look out the window. Jean relaxed, comforted by their joint acceptance of him as a person who knew things they wanted to know.

Sitting on Some of the Benches

As the shuttle neared their destination, Jean spoke to Luisa and Emille. "If I remember correctly, Mr. Monet's house is pink with white trim around the front door and some windows. However, one would never notice the white or pink because Mr. Monet has established green as the color to see. The steps to the front door, the front door itself, the shutters on the windows, and two benches on the sidewalk in front of the door are all the same deep green.

Boston ivy and roses are fixed to a trellis. Geraniums of pink and red seem to be everywhere, except for silver carnation blossoms.

"There are other benches, also green in color, located at nice spots among the gardens because Mr. Monet believes in having places for himself as well as his visitors to sit and enjoy the light and color of the gardens. I do that when I can, though he keeps me busy gardening. He also expects me to be painting. To tell the truth, Mr. Monet appreciates when someone sits on a bench in his garden. But not if the person is working for him or has an assignment as his student."

"You clearly love plants and gardens, from what you have told us. I look forward to sitting on some of the benches," Luisa said, leaning toward the window in obvious anticipation. "And learning more about painting, of course."

"Me too," Emille said. "But why green? And why green everywhere? Doesn't he have enough green in his gardens?"

"Ask him," Jean said, clapping his hands. "There is more. This green paint is matched by a large planting of nasturtiums of the same color on the other side of the walk. Mr. Monet wanted to soften the straight lines of the path, which the nasturtiums do nicely. Different plants also line the path at different places, like irises, to give more variety. Can you imagine painting his garden, since you haven't seen it yet? Green dominates most gardens. Actually, that's a good question to ask yourself and your friend. Figuring out why a great artist picks a specific color will help your art learning." He hoped they wouldn't let their preconceived ideas prevent them from learning from the great artist.

Emille asked Jean what a nasturtium looked like and added, "Don't just say it is a plant."

"Not just a plant. Okay. It is a green plant. Big leaves that smell great. And flowers at times that pop up with a variety of color. You'll see."

Luisa straightened her skirt and then smiled at Emille. "Jean, you seem to know a lot about garden plants, and you obviously remember a lot about the house and the gardens. Why? Does Mr. Monet teach that to you? Will he teach it to us?"

"The simple answer is that I lived there, in housing for the gardeners, for two years and did a lot of work on the buildings as well as the gardens. But really, I am remembering as an artist, not as a gardener. Well, that too. I learn what he wants me to learn, so I can do what he wants done. But remember, Mr. Monet is an artist who does everything with art in mind. Everything. Art in mind, body, and soul. His kitchen, for example, has blue-and-white tiles made in the nearby town of Rouen. Painted at the factory by hand. Blue and white with different patterns. Mr. Monet selected the tiles and arranged them to match the kitchen and its blue walls to complement the two-toned yellow dining room. The salon, by the way, is white with blue trim. I hope we get to talk with Mr. Monet in that room, at least when we're in a lesson."

The shuttle lurched a bit. "Looks like we're here. The driver must have figured out we're here to see Mr. Monet. May I get off first so I can help you ladies as you get off with your baggage?"

The shuttle driver opened the door, and the ladies easily left Jean sitting on his seat. He leaned forward and eased himself out of the shuttle. The ladies had waited for him, so the three of them walked down a path over to where Mr. Monet stood by his easel. Luisa gently put her arm around Emille's shoulders as they walked together. Emille looked at her and smiled. Jean liked their friendship, impressed that they had met only a few days ago.

That's the River Sort of Close to Here, Isn't It?

When they got to Mr. Monet and his easel, he frowned directly at the two ladies until Luisa took her arm off Emille and stepped to the side. Monet wore a tan coat with a fur collar, a hat with feathers, and pants of the same color as the coat. Then he saw Jean and smiled, waving him up to his easel. "Jean, how are you? Are you ready to work?" They shook hands, and then Monet pointed to the garden. "We just got a delivery of nasturtiums over there. Go see the others, and they'll tell you what to do. I want that project finished today. I've got other plans for tomorrow."

Emille looked at the plants Monet had pointed to and then nodded in affirmation to Jean.

With a wave, Monet dismissed Jean, who then leaned around the artist to see what he had painted. Jean saw trees—seven, he quickly counted. Each rose straight up from what looked like the bank of a river. "Claude, that's the river close to here, isn't it? I think I've seen this clump of trees."

"Yes. This is along the River Epte, near where it enters the River Seine. You can look at it later. I'm trying something new, and we can talk about it." Monet stared at Jean and then at the path that led to where the gardeners were working.

Jean shrugged and walked toward the other gardeners. Emille and Luisa moved over to see the painting also. Jean heard Luisa introduce them to Monet, and he smiled when she mentioned that both of them were from Pennsylvania but from different suburbs and had met just more than a week ago. She added that they both had come to learn from him. He also noticed that Emille looked back at him twice, so when he got to the plants, he picked up one of the nasturtiums so she could get a better view of it. She gave him a quick wave of thanks.

Also, when Jean got to the gardeners, he spoke to Leon Duret and Georges Origo, two men he remembered working with. Leon and Jean had become friends, and both enjoyed their reunion. They spoke of sharing some wine soon, perhaps that night. That idea appealed to Jean. Two of the others, Carlo Mangan and Arnold Andraud, introduced themselves to him. He felt their welcome, and they talked for a bit. A third other gardener stood facing away from Jean with his arms folded. They all could see Monet looking at them, interrupting his talk with the ladies. Jean learned that Monet planned to have them divert a stream from the River Epte. He also learned that several neighbors were not happy about it.

The neighbors were afraid the new plants Monet brought in would harm their farm crops. Jean laughed because he knew Monet bought growing plants, like the nasturtiums they were to plant.

The task for that day consisted of planting the huge pile of nasturtiums along the new path where they were standing. The gardeners had just started planting on one side. Taller flowers filled both sides of the path, giving a rainbow of color. The nasturtiums would transition the tan wood chips on the path to the flowers.

Jean picked up a shovel and started digging small holes in the soil, while Leon put nasturtium plants into the holes, and Carlo packed the soil and put water on the plants. The others worked the other side in the same manner. Jean enjoyed the rhythm of their work and told Leon his back remembered that kind of work.

When they'd finished, the gardeners cleaned up, and Jean cleaned himself before he went looking for the ladies.

We Would Learn a Lot about Color

Emille and Luisa were standing close to the painting, each pointing out a feature to the other. "Out of my way," Monet said loudly. "I need to work on this while the light is right. Are you artists? Artist wannabes?"

Both ladies moved away from the painting, and Luisa asked him, "Isn't this a painting of some other place? Near a river?"

"Well, yes. It is. That's what I just told Jean. Didn't you hear me? Do you ladies know him?"

"No," Emille replied. "We introduced ourselves to him on the shuttle coming here. I see there are a few trees near here that you can use as you complete the painting."

"Right. Now, go wander through the gardens. I'll talk to you later, when the sunlight changes. Do either of you have an instructor?"

"No," Luisa said, thinking she should take her turn to talk to Monet. "We met Mr. Degas briefly for a lesson and understand he is teaching Mary Cassatt. She is also from a Philadelphia suburb. It's different from either of our suburbs. We also talked with Mr. Degas in a café in Paris where a lot of artists hang out. Oh, and I saw a painting by you of a haystack."

"Study it," Monet said as he continued to work. "Or buy it when you get back there. You will learn a lot. Now, go walk in the gardens. I'll give you some time later, like I said." He flashed his elbows as if to brush them away and keep them from standing too close to the canvas. Then he started, looking and quickly stroking with his brush.

Both ladies curtsied and then watched Monet paint. He ignored them since he now could stand in front of the painting. The ladies didn't understand his quick glance at the tree and then the quick few strokes of his brush. Still, both could see the tree coming alive and said so. Then they began walking on the path into the gardens. When they were out of Monet's sight, Luisa put her arm around Emille's shoulders again. They stopped in awe of a tall rosebush hung on a rack of supports on top of a base or stem. The rosebush had climbed taller than the ladies stood. They went to the base, where they pointed out irises, peonies, and other flowers. Emille laughed as she said she felt tempted to pick some of the flowers but wouldn't until she had a vase or two. Luisa wondered if Mr. Monet put flowers in vases or if his wife did.

They walked for a while longer, pointing out plants and flowers to each other, and then sat on a green bench near a wall of the house. "Mr. Monet is a wonderful gardener," Luisa said. "I know you know that. He's also a great painter, and we both know that as well. I'm saying what I said about him to myself as well as to you. But what do you think about him? Monet himself?"

"I agree he's great at what he does. Plus, he didn't come on to either of us. I've heard rumors, but they may have been started by people jealous of his art. In fact, he seemed gruff. Like the way he told Jean to go to work. But I'm going to buy that painting at the café."

"Not if I buy it first," Luisa said, laughing. "We can share it. We have a lot in common. But we are not going to share Jean.

Sorry. My sense of humor has gotten the best of me. I didn't mean anything by that."

"Well, Luisa, just think about the gardens. If they had frames, you could call them paintings. In one place, he has a solid color from identical plants. In other places, the variety of plants and their colors defy description. The flower beds are so dense. I think that is the word." Emille leaned back as if to surrender to the beauty.

"I suspect we would learn a lot about color if we tried to paint some of these gardens you just described. I do mean learn, because I don't know how I could paint the variety of color in one place and the solid single color in another place. How could I show the leaves in a wall of green, say? Do you think that part of our instructions will be painting the gardens? Let's ask him. Well now, we need to walk the gardens again nearer to sunset to see what the changed light does to these gardens."

They were both silent then, looking out at the gardens before them. Neither seemed to be able to describe the details of the gardens. They were surprised to be making plans together so soon after meeting.

Emille looked up at the blue sky and the variety of shapes of white clouds. "In my youth, I would lie on the grass in our backyard and look up at the clouds. I could recognize the shapes of different things, like rabbits or horses. You know what I mean?" She held her hands up to her eyebrows to prevent the sun from keeping her from seeing the clouds.

"Yes, I do, Emille. I also did that, and to tell the truth, I could do that now. Just looking up from this bench won't do it. I need to be on my back on a lawn. If there is any lawn here."

Eventually, they wandered back to where they had met Monet.

Looking Down the Path

Every time he had the chance, Jean tried to watch Monet when he was painting. He had cleaned up after his work in the garden.

He stopped as he approached the artist, simply enjoying Monet at work. He also felt he would remember past lessons better by watching Monet paint. When Monet noticed Jean had come back, he knew that by simply watching, Jean couldn't learn technique, as he would later when standing at an easel next to Monet or talking with him. Still, he hoped Jean would learn something then or at least have his memory refreshed.

Jean looked at the man who would teach him more. Monet had lost most of his hair as he approached his sixtieth year of age. He smiled, knowing he probably would do the same. Monet had strong eyebrows, a full gray—almost white—beard, and a black mustache. When the skin between his eyebrows made a ridge, it looked somewhat like an exclamation point. His beard kept those talking with him from seeing his smile, if he had one. He often wore a wide-brimmed tan hat to protect himself from the sun when he painted outdoors, which was nearly all the time. Average in height, he did not project the power one might have expected after seeing his paintings. The power could be seen, however, if one watched him paint.

"Jean!" Monet called to him. "Come here. I want to show you something."

Jean went quickly to him, not wanting anything to distract him. That was how he had learned from him. "What is it, Mr. Monet?" Jean immediately felt embarrassed for making the same mistake again.

"If you don't start calling me Claude, I won't talk to you at all." He glared at Jean for a moment. "Look at this, where the trees are reflected in the creek. I painted one like this back in the fifties, and I'm going to change these reflections to how I now see them."

The light from the sun reflected off the river water onto the trees and between them toward the viewer. The sky seemed normal, but the sunlight made the scene come alive. Jean felt the painting reach out to him, inviting him to look closer. Jean had never considered having sunlight reflect off water. "Mr., ah,

Claude, it is really interesting to see you take a painting from more than thirty years ago, when you were my age, and bring it into the present time. I like the way the water flows."

"That's good. Because you and the other gardeners are going to bring some of that water here. I want ponds. I've already ordered water lilies and found out how to plant them. Do you want to know how?"

"Not now. I'm sure you'll explain it thoroughly when it is time to plant them." Jean could picture the instructions: Monet would be standing on the bank, elevated over the gardeners, having Jean or another gardener demonstrate whatever instructions he had.

"I see you have been looking down the path. Waiting for the ladies?"

"You are quite observant, Claude. I just met them, so I don't know much about either lady. Which one should I date first?"

"You might have to date both lovely ladies at the same time, as I see it. Here they come. Good luck. I'll say more later."

Jean straightened his collar and made sure his shirt hadn't bunched up in front to hide his trim stomach. Monet pointed at him and laughed and then resumed painting.

I'll Dance with You

Walking along, still out of sight of Monet, Emille stepped away from Luisa and then pirouetted on one foot, holding her arms out. "These gardens make me want to dance. I love them so."

"I'll dance with you," Luisa said, moving to her.

"No, I like to dance alone." She did another pirouette. Her arms seemed to function as wings as she danced. She stopped and looked at Luisa, now willing to listen to her friend as she spoke.

"We haven't shared much about ourselves," Luisa said. "Are you married? You don't have a wedding ring, but neither do I. Do you have a boyfriend? Or maybe I should say a gentlemen friend?"

"No. Neither. Do you?" Emille clasped her hands, hiding her left hand. "No ring and no desire to have one." She bowed to Luisa.

"No. Where did you go to school? I went to Bryn Mawr College. I studied painting, watercolor, and sketches. I didn't like it because they wanted views of Philadelphia for historical records, and I wanted to do portraits. But I did learn some technique, like in what I showed you on the train."

"I failed at college. What I mean is that I applied to the University of Pennsylvania, and it rejected me. They weren't letting women in back then and still don't, I think. I went to the Pennsylvania Academy of Fine Arts. Mary Cassatt studied there too but many years before me. I feel I learned to paint but nothing academic. Now I want to paint gardens," Emille said, pirouetting again. "I wonder if I can dance with a brush in my hands. Can I stop in the right place to dab on some color like we've seen Monet do? Oh, I know his skill is knowing where to put the dab. Do you think I, or we, can learn where each dab should go? I still don't see what he sees."

Luisa moved closer to her dancing friend. "I don't know the answer to that. To put it bluntly, my gut reaction is that we will succeed. I believe in gut reactions."

"Luisa, I don't mind you using that word that I won't say. But I don't believe in those reactions, even though I have them. I just don't believe them."

"Emille, I still think you should dance with me."

Emille waltzed away. They continued to walk along the paths in the garden, eventually coming to the back of Monet's house. They stopped and looked up at the second floor. Emille began to sketch the house.

"I think that is his wife's bedroom," Luisa said, pointing to a window. "Monet and his wife sleep in different rooms. Degas told me. My parents do too. It's what cool married people do. We could do that. I mean when we travel or are staying somewhere for art lessons. We could save money doing that."

As they crossed the road, a young man called out to them and came up, smiling. "Hello, ladies. My name is Pierre Stéphane. Remember me from the train ride from Paris, when I tried to talk to you? I'm studying to be an artist, and I figure you are also artists. Isn't this a wonderful place?"

Luisa curtsied, saying, "Yes, it is wonderful, and yes, we are artists. We are here to speak with Mr. Monet. Perhaps we'll see you later." She started to walk to the front of the house.

"May I take your arm as we walk? I want to be a gentleman."

"Not now and not ever," Emille replied. "Neither of us is interested." She whispered to Luisa "He comes on strong. Not like Jean."

The ladies moved toward each other to keep him away.

A Starving Artist

Monet and Jean were sitting on a green bench when the ladies came into sight. They hurried over to Monet and stopped just in front of him. Emille paused to look at Monet's painting, smiling as she saw the light on the tree trunks. It's beautiful.

"Thank you, miss." Monet got up from the bench. "Have you made arrangements for the night here in Giverny?"

Emille stepped over to stand next to Luisa. "Yes, we've booked two rooms at the hotel in town. It is not far, is it?"

"I'll escort you," Pierre said, coming up to them.

He came closer to them, and Emille waved him away. "No. I told you neither of us is interested. Neither of us. Understand?" Both ladies turned their backs on Pierre.

He continued to talk. "I just want you to be safe. I'll come back here when you get inside your hotel or wherever you are staying." Rather than looking at the ladies, Pierre looked at Jean, then at Monet, and then up at the sky.

"I'll see they are safe," Monet said, "and maybe you should figure out where you are staying. And as far as safety is concerned, people around here are fine. They leave you alone." He pointed at Pierre. "Ladies, let us go into my house for a meal. Oh, Jean, you can come in also." Monet didn't even look at Pierre.

The four of them went up the green stairs to the main entrance and then to the dining room, which Monet had painted in two shades of yellow. The women noticed the framed art on the walls and saw how the yellows made the room feel as if he had exposed it to the bathing sun. Jean commented on a print by Utamaro, one of the best of many Japanese artists whose works Monet collected.

"I just got that last month. Hokusai and Hiroshige are my other two favorites. Ladies, please seat yourselves on that side so you can face the kitchen. You will see the blue kitchen is nicely contrasted with this dining room when the door is open. Jean, you sit at the foot. I will be at the head of the table."

They all took their assigned seats. Jean joined them in looking around at the decorations. He tried to understand the Utamaro print, particularly the relationship of the man to the woman. He wished the wine would be served as soon as possible.

Monet did not have to call to the kitchen for service. His wife, Alice, came in through the kitchen door and took her place next to Monet on one side of the table, with her back to the kitchen. She told him the server would bring in the food soon. Then Alice said, "Claude, some guy named Pierre came to the kitchen door and begged for some food. He said he wanted to become an artist."

"A starving artist," Monet said. No one else laughed. "I'll look at his art later."

When the server brought the food to the table, Monet told her to give the beggar some food but to tell him it was the only time he would get anything. "Oh, and tell him that I want to see his artwork." As the server left, he said, "And after this meal, ladies, I will look at your art, if you have any. I might do a bit more. Alice, bless the food."

Alice began with the sign of the cross and then asked the Virgin Mary to bless the food. She ended with the sign of the cross again. Monet and Jean bowed their heads during the prayer. Both ladies sat with hands clasped in prayer.

No one spoke during the meal. Monet took two servings of everything and preferred not to talk with his mouth full. At the end, Emille asked to be introduced to his wife. Monet made the introduction after asking the ladies to introduce themselves, since he had forgotten their names. He also apologized for his failure to be a proper host. Alice nodded to Jean, as she remembered him from his work in the gardens and his painting.

She Held It Up for Him to See

After the delicious meal of baked chicken with a spicy sauce and a lettuce salad, Monet, Jean, Luisa, and Emille went back outside,

leaving Alice to her duties. The two ladies praised the meal as they
followed Monet to the benches. Jean had hoped to go to the blue
sitting room in the house, where Monet often had conversations
with artists, collectors, and dealers. Instead, they sat on the green
benches, as they had before dinner. Jean wondered if they were
outside on the benches because Monet wanted to emphasize
outdoor as the place to do art. Monet asked to see their art. Pierre
walked up, licking his lips. He obviously had eaten what Monet and
his guests had eaten, meaning he'd eaten quite well.

"Well, if it isn't the starving artist. Do you have some of your
work?"

"Thank you, Mr. Monet, for the wonderful meal. Yes, I have
some here in this bag." Pierre hugged his bag.

"Ladies first. Sit down and relax. Thank you for your polite
comments on our dinner. That won't change what you were to be
told. No more handouts. By the way, we eat that way all the time.
Now, which of you lovely ladies will be going first? Let me see your
work as an artist. Or as one who wants to be an artist."

Both ladies slumped at Monet's tone of voice. Then Luisa
unrolled a canvas showing a landscape, with two ladies on a
blanket in an open area by some woods. "Mr. Monet, I understand
you painted something like this, with more ladies and some men."
She held it up for him to see.

Monet looked at the canvas, moved his head from one side to
the other, and then waved her away. He knew which painting she
referred to, but he shook his head. "I don't approve of anyone saying
they painted something like I did. Look at your trees. They're
solid. The women aren't even looking at each other, let alone in
conversation. You flunk." He dismissed her with a wave of his arm
and then looked at Emille to see what she would show him.

Jean felt both surprised and pleased that Monet had made
a reference to the placement of the ladies in the painting.
Composition was important, though Monet could have asked
Luisa if she planned to do more before expressing his disapproval

of the painting. Jean got a glance at Luisa's artwork, noting that Monet had focused on the layout of the ladies and the landscape, not saying anything about the painting technique. He thought about some of the lessons he'd had two years ago and felt sorry for the embarrassment the ladies would likely face in the lessons to come. He needed to tell them to suffer in silence and do what Monet told them to do. It would get better.

Luisa rolled up her painting and put it back in her bag. Tears were running down her cheeks. She looked at Jean. "Degas must have known."

Emille went over to her and held her by the shoulders. Then she turned to Monet. "Mr. Monet, we came to Giverny to have you teach us something, not to be flunked. You won't like my artwork either, so I'm not even going to show it to you."

Jean stood up and held up his hand to Monet. "On the shuttle, they asked me what you would think of their art. I replied that I wanted to know what their instructor had told them. They said Degas told them not to show it. I should have told them that this happened to me as well some years ago."

Jean had felt he had to say something, but Monet didn't even acknowledge his presence. Monet got up from the bench and looked at each aspiring artist. "Wait here, ladies, and don't even think of leaving." He stomped off to the studio where he kept his paints and art supplies. Both ladies stood where they were, sharing their pain.

Jean tried to think of something to say and then remembered what had happened to him when he'd shown his early art to Monet. "It's okay. Calm down. I know you feel insulted and worse, like I did when I went through this. But he went to his studio back then, just like now, and he brought out a small canvas and told me to draw a hay bale. He gave me some charcoal. See? Here he comes now with some canvases. This is a great opportunity. I just hope I get a canvas too."

Luisa turned away from Monet as he approached, but Emille stared at him.

What Happened the Next Morning?

Monet walked up to Jean and the two ladies and gave each of them a canvas and a charcoal stick. Then he turned to address them. "Do you know about perspective? I mean really know and understand perspective?"

Each lady took a canvas but quickly held it behind her. Both looked around and at each other. Jean stood tall, and they stared at him. What did he know that they didn't?

They all said they understood perspective, and Monet told Jean to be quiet. "You can draw when the time comes, but let's let the ladies take their turn at learning. Ladies, do you understand perspective?" He looked around, frowned, and then said, "You," pointing to Luisa. "Point to some perspective that we can see, please."

Luisa turned to face Monet's house. When she pointed to the house, her hand shook. "See how the roof line at the far end of your house seems lower than the close end? It isn't lower, but perspective makes things smaller at a longer distance. Look at the path. If it were long enough, it would come to a point, but even now, we can see the sides getting closer together. They aren't moving, but that is perspective." She hesitated and then added, "Do you understand?" She looked at Emille as if she needed a hug and wanted to be held closely. Jean almost volunteered to provide the hug.

"Why do you ask if I understand? I'm an artist. Look at my paintings of haystacks, for example. There is no train track, but any fool can see the perspective."

Jean felt he needed to jump in because Monet didn't have the enthusiasm for the ladies that he'd had for Jean not so many years ago. "Mr. Monet, we can all see the perspective. Please share with us the point to looking for it."

"Jean, if you don't call me Claude, you can leave this group of people wishing they were artists." Monet turned to his left to present himself to the ladies and not to Jean.

"Claude, I'm here to learn from you," Jean said. "From my perspective, if you don't mind my using that word, I want to learn."

Monet shook his head and then sat back on the bench. "Jean, I wish you had not said that word in that way. I want to get these ladies to understand that perspective is not just about train tracks. It is even more important to discover and understand what each of us, as an artist, has in our eyes and minds when we paint or draw. What is our personal perspective that has us see the light and the color of what we are putting on the canvas? I want each of you to draw a tree. Any tree on the property. Do it now, and draw the same tree in the morning, before or right after you eat breakfast. Draw the same tree twice from your own perspective but at quite different times of day. That's all for now. I have things to do. And you do as well. Get busy." Monet walked back to the studio, ignoring requests from Luisa for more instruction.

Pierre sprawled on the bench, holding his head with both hands. Emille asked him if he felt okay.

"I am in ecstasy. I'm going to spend the night looking for my perspective." He got off the bench and went down the path, swaying back and forth, still holding his head.

Emille turned to Jean. "You have not been open with us. But thank you for bringing Mr. Monet back to his point: our perspectives. Will we survive like you did? Is this what happened to you?"

"Similar. I had to draw a haystack twice, as with this assignment. I spent so much time on the light and color that the stack itself looked terrible."

"What happened the next morning?"

"I had breakfast. Sorry. That's not funny. Actually, Mr. Monet took my two sketches and marked them up, almost destroying the canvas. He—well, *redrew* is not a strong enough word. But he showed me how I had not properly observed light and color and had totally ignored how the sun changed the way the haystack looked in his eyes—and my eyes, once I saw what he meant. It amazed me, as our starving artist said it amazed him, but only after Mr. Monet, or Claude, brought them to light, if I can use that word. He changed my perspective on art."

"Thank you, Mr. Jean. Emille and I need to find our tree now."

"Before you go, there is something else Claude taught me. Emille, give me your hand. I see you have had it in your pocket, so it should be warm." He took her hand in his. "I hope your hand is as warm as mine is cold."

"I feel your coldness. Do you feel my warmth?" Emille said without blushing.

"Yes. Now, do it with your own hand and arm. Do you feel both warm and cold?"

Luisa asked to hold Emille's hand instead of Jean's. Then she did it to herself and felt both warm and cold.

Emille asked, "What does this mean?"

Luisa said, "Why did you get us to feel both hot and cold?"

"Ladies, it is a way to remember what and where. A painter looks at not only what is being applied to the canvas but also where, which means one must be aware of what is on the brush as well as what is on the canvas. Mr. Monet will teach you this. He liked my use of hot and cold. Be surprised if you can."

The women stood there looking at him as if he had opened the heavens for them. They nodded and then went down the path to find a tree. They knew they had to paint the tree soon, but they were overwhelmed, as they so much to process. Knowing Jean had had a similar experience and survived as a student of Monet gave them hope—and fear.

The ladies had more fear when they heard a huge roar coming from the house. "What is that?" Luisa shouted. They ran to Jean, and each grabbed an arm.

"Relax, ladies. You can keep holding my arms, but relax. The noise, which is getting farther away, is Mr. Monet driving one of his steam cars. He's probably going to Rouen. He has painted the cathedral there quite a few times. The different times of day produce different shadows and colors, like with the hay bales."

The ladies let him go and stepped back. Luisa sat down on the green bench, and Emille looked at her blank canvas and said, "Time to find a tree to paint."

I See What You Are Doing with the Sun

Monet indeed drove toward Rouen in his three-wheeled 1888 Serpollet steam car. He often said that a fast ride through the countryside helped him appreciate his gardens and home in Giverny. Nothing, even the mansions he saw along the ride, had the completeness he had built since moving there. He told Alice the drives affirmed his decisions about the gardens as well as his paintings. Alice replied that she would not ride with him at any speed and certainly not as fast as he drove. Her refusal never ended.

In Rouen, he pulled his car into a parking place directly across from the Cathédrale Notre-Dame de Rouen. Monet had already made twenty-seven paintings of the huge building, which had been the tallest building in the world only ten years ago. He went inside a little store that had a large window and door, both with curtains. A single counter displayed goods for sale, with a rack below the glass top, on which ice could be put for keeping fish or meat cool. Monet had no interest in what was in the room and barely looked around. He walked over to the stairway to the second floor and went up. That was where he painted the cathedral over and over under different lighting conditions.

By the one window on the second floor was an easel on which a painting in progress faced the window. He pulled the curtain aside to view the building. Monet kept the location of that studio secret, not wanting others, especially artists, to know where his location for the project was.

He ignored the rest of the makeshift studio. The back of the first floor had nothing except a door that overlooked a park. Monet felt curious about the park. It had paths and trees, as one would have expected, but also had far more benches than he thought would be needed.

As he opened a tube of paint, he heard a knock on the door to the street. He went back down the stairs and opened the door to find a Catholic priest wearing a long-sleeved black robe that extended down to his black shoes.

"Mr. Monet?" the priest asked. When Monet nodded, he said, "My name is Monsignor Jacques Hamel. I am the priest at the cathedral you have been painting. May I come in?"

"Of course. Do come in. What can I do for you? Oh, and I don't have much time because the light is just where I need it." Monet pointed to the stairs where he would go back to the easel and start making his palette. The two of them went up to the second floor.

Father Hamel stood behind Monet and watched him paint a part of the cathedral that didn't have sun on it. "I came by to meet you and to thank you for what you are doing for our congregation. Have you looked out your back door?"

"Yes, and why are there so many benches in the park?" Monet put some yellow on the wall next to the shaded part.

"I had them put there. Our congregation includes many people who want to talk about their faith with others or solve some problem in their lives by getting advice from another parishioner. Some simply like to talk with their fellow members. The sanctuary is not a place for conversations with other people. There we talk to God."

Monet continued to paint, not saying anything. To himself, he thought he would enjoy being part of a conversation with the priest and the writer Zola. *Who would be the first to walk out? Zola would for sure, after his lecture to the priest.*

"Mr. Monet, are you Catholic?"

"In my youth, Father, but like so many of us, I don't attend church. But my wife, Alice, is a good Catholic who does go to church. We pray together at home. What I like and don't like about Catholics is that they tell you what your sin is. Her priest said Alice and I couldn't get married until her former husband died. And we did wait. Her priest said she remained married in his eyes because the man still lived. I told him to get his eyes checked and start by looking at our bed. Alice still goes to church, and I forget why I don't."

Father Hamel apparently decided not to comment. "I see what you are doing with the sun, Mr. Monet. I will let you work without my distracting conversation. May God bless you and continue to inspire your work as an artist and as a gardener, I'm told. Perhaps I will visit your gardens sometime during the season if that is reasonable for you."

"Thank you, Father, for coming to meet me and for leaving while I work. Yes, you should visit my gardens. I will also make sure you get one of these paintings. I hope it will be one for a brighter day."

The priest left after blessing Monet, and Monet left when he had finished his work on the painting as the sunlight changed. He did not go to a park bench.

Ask Me to Reconsider My Choice

After leaving Jean when they could no longer hear Monet's car, Luisa and Emille walked side by side down the path. Neither spoke for a while, but each pointed to trees along the path as potential candidates for the assignment. They came to a clump of five poplar trees and stopped.

"Hey, why don't we each pick a tree from these?" Emille said. "I like—"

"Don't pick a tree yet," Luisa said. "I think we should draw the same tree. That way, Monet will not only see that we paint differently, but we will each get our own opinion from him as well as learn something from the other's opinion. These five are the best trees we've seen so far. They belong to us."

"Well, maybe. Oh yes, they're the best so far, and I don't want to look anymore. But only if I can pick the tree for both of us."

"Who put you in charge?" Luisa moved next to Emille and looked at the five trees from her perspective. "I know what we can do. I'll eliminate one tree, then you eliminate the next one, and I'll eliminate the next one. There will be two trees left, and you pick between them. That could be more fun. You like fun, don't you?"

Emille stepped a bit closer to the trees. She looked at each of them. "I know which one I want. What if you reject it? That's not fun."

"Okay, my dear, if I reject your favorite, ask me to reconsider my choice. My first pick will be from all five trees, and the other one will be from three. You have a great chance that way, or, as my father would say, great odds. But if I reject your favorite, I will reconsider. But I will have the right to keep my choice after I explain why. Regardless, the odds are greatly in your favor. By the way, my father does not gamble."

"Okay, Luisa, I see this as a way for both of us to have input. I like this thinking. We're partners in this project. Oh, and I neglected to affirm your suggestion that we both draw the same tree. I like your reasoning. So from left to right, they are numbers one, two, three, four, and five."

"Number two is out." Luisa spoke without looking at the trees.

"Number three is out." Emille did the same, knowing which one she'd picked.

"Number five is out." Luisa clapped her hands.

"Yes! My pick is number one, so number four is out. I like the way my tree leans toward the setting sun more than the others. And the bark is interesting." Emille smiled. "Interesting."

"Interesting is right. Remember, now it's your tree and my tree. Let's get to work before we run out of sunlight." Luisa held up her charcoal stick and began to draw the tree. "Oh, and we'll leave the other trees out of our drawings, yes?"

"Yes," Emille replied as she began to draw her tree her way.

After they'd finished their drawings, both commented on how the sun, which was now setting, had changed the look of the tree even as they'd worked on it. They looked down the path and saw Monet coming toward them.

When he reached the ladies, he said, "I want some exercise, so I will walk you to your hotel. Jean will meet you there in the morning to bring you back here. And don't forget to bring your canvas to redraw the same tree."

"We won't forget," they both said, and they fell in line behind him.

When their hotel came into view, Monet pointed to it and said good night. The ladies said good night too.

Kind Is Not His Way of Teaching

The next morning, Jean got to their hotel just as Luisa and Emille were coming onto the large front porch, each with a cup of tea in hand. "Do you mind if I get a cup and join you?" he asked as he climbed the three steps to the porch. They nodded.

He put his bag on a chair and then quickly went inside and got his tea. He sat across from them, as he had in the shuttle yesterday. Turning to the side, he put his feet up on the chair next to him. "A lot has happened since our ride together to Giverny."

No one thought it necessary to list the events.

Both ladies were silent, sipping their tea. Then Luisa spoke. "Jean, tell us—what will happen today? Will Mr. Monet be kind?"

Emille continued looking away at a garden.

Jean could see they both were tense, leading him to think they were dreading the session with Monet. "Being kind is not his way of teaching," he said, hoping to convince the two ladies to take what happened as part of the learning experience. "There are other fine artists in Montmartre and the rest of Paris. You've met Degas. He's a kind teacher. Besides, you want to learn from the best, even if the artist is not kind. Think about it." As he thought about what he'd said, he realized he had voiced his own perspective on being taught art. "That's my perspective," he added.

Both ladies smiled but did not laugh at his perspective comment. Emille excused herself, saying she would be back with both canvases and charcoal sticks.

Luisa took a sip of her tea. "Yes, Mr. Degas is a kind teacher. And at least he warned us about Mr. Monet. What will happen today?"

"It all depends on each of our canvases. Which reminds me that we should get on our way while we have strong morning light."

Emille came out, handed a canvas to Luisa, and started down the steps. Luisa joined her, and they began walking. Jean quickly finished his tea and joined them. He saw that they had paid attention to the route when Monet had brought them to the hotel.

He tried to get between them, wanting to have a lady on each arm, but couldn't. The Philadelphian ladies remained obviously quite formal. Both avoided any contact with him. When they got close to Giverny, they started looking for their tree.

"Goodbye, Mr. Jean," Luisa said, turning onto a path that eventually led to Monet's house. He continued walking ahead, needing to find his tree. He paused, watching them go down their path and then stop, both pointing to a clump of poplar trees just into the garden next to the path. When they both held up their canvases, he knew they would be fine. He also hoped their sketches would be acceptable to Monet.

He found his tree and took his canvas out of his bag. He could see how the morning sunlight made it bright, reflecting a vivid yellow back at him. He looked again to be sure he had the same tree. When he'd finished his drawing, he could see the difference the sun had caused between yesterday and that day. *I'll do fine*, he thought, and he went to the house to find the others.

Luisa and Emille were already there, sitting on the green bench by the front door. Monet sat opposite them on the other bench. When Jean sat on the bench with the ladies, they both moved a symbolic bit away from him.

Monet took Emille's canvas first, as Jean had thought he would after remembering her refusal to show him her work yesterday. Monet kept track of how he was treated.

After a few moments of study, Monet asked, "Why, even though it appears to be the same tree, does your drawing show the tree from two opposite angles?"

"I wanted the sun to shine on the tree from the same direction, showing sunset and sunrise. Is that bad?"

Monet frowned. "I should have been more explicit. I wanted to see how you handled light from two directions on the same side of the tree. Your showing light on two sides doesn't let me do that." He dropped the canvas onto the ground. "You get no critique." He turned to Luisa. "And you, my lady. May I see your canvas?"

"Of course, Mr. Monet. Here," Luisa said as she gave him her canvas.

Monet smiled as he looked at the drawings. "Same side of the tree, different sources of light. That's good. The drawings are not good. Neither shows how the light strikes the tree from yesterday and how the light defines the tree from today. See how, for example, the light should have been directly on the trunk and branches? See how it isn't? This is no good either." He dropped the canvas onto the ground.

Each lady picked up her canvas and walked away, saying nothing, presumably going to the hotel to get their bags. They soon would be on their way back to Paris. Jean thought they kept the canvases as souvenirs—not to remember but simply to show off.

Rather Than Be a Wife and All That

After they collected their luggage, the ride in the shuttle felt uneventful for Luisa and Emille. They rode facing the direction of travel. This time, no one sat facing them, and both spent much of the trip just looking at the countryside. They did not say anything about the failed lesson. Emille took out her canvas and tried to remember how the light had shone in the morning, hoping to complete the assignment. Luisa simply looked out the window, her canvas face down on her lap.

The train ride back to Paris and the Saint-Lazare station gave them more of the same. Emille had her chance to sit next to the window on the train as they had agreed on the trip to Giverney. She looked at her drawing occasionally but did not change the canvas Monet had rejected. She told herself over and over that his was just one art teacher's opinion. She thought about Degas. Would he continue to teach her? Would he introduce her to Mary Cassatt? What about Luisa? *We're friends and a lot closer than I would have expected after just getting to know each other.* She laughed when she thought about Boston marriages.

"What's so funny?" Luisa said. She held her canvas up for her friend to see. "I haven't figured out how to make the tree like Monet wanted and like he paints them. I can see what I want but don't know how to put it on the canvas. Maybe we should have stayed and taken our torture. Jean must have done that because he has learned the technique. Anyway, what were you laughing at?"

"I have been thinking about us. You and me. We've only known each other a short time. We've had one lesson from Degas, and we've had this trip to Giverny. Do you think we will be able to work together and actually look out for each other? We don't really understand Paris, let alone Montmartre. Jean could help if he didn't stay back with Monet, playing at being a gardener." Emille turned to look at the other passengers in the train car and sighed.

"Yes, Jean," Luisa said. "I glanced at his canvas, and it was very much like what Monet wanted us to do. Of course, he's been through all this before." Both ladies paused to look out the train window at a field of haystacks. "Look at that, Emille. Monet is speaking to us as we return to Paris."

"Maybe it's Jean speaking to us here."

"Emille, do you like him? I mean, oh, romantically. He is good looking, and he's French and an artist. For what that might be worth."

"No. Do you?"

"No. No romance for him." Luisa looked at Emille, giving her a smile and a frown. "When I heard you laugh, I was wondering if you were going to bring up a Boston marriage. You know what they are?"

"Yes, Luisa, I do. That is why I laughed. I met Gabrielle de Veaux Clements and Ellen Day Hale briefly at an art show. Both are artists who met each other about ten years ago. They travel together. My art instructor back home said the two women artists are establishing a home together. They might come to Paris while we're here. Clements was born in Philadelphia, but what they are living is called a Boston marriage."

"That's how I understand their relationship. As a matter of fact, I have a cousin from Boston who explained that Boston marriages encompass a wide variety of relationships. They could be lovers, or they could be totally uninterested in a romantic relationship with each other. Some live together like that so they can have careers, like being artists or working in medicine. Actually, anything rather than being a wife and all that."

Draw It First, and Then Paint It

After the ladies left Monet at his easel, Jean waited for him to relax. Monet kept pacing, frowning, and sticking his lips out as if to hide his teeth. Jean focused on his canvas, which Monet had not examined. Seeing it, Monet said, "Jean, give it to me." After a moment's review, he handed it back to him. "You have done well. Much better than last time you showed me a picture with light. You will make it after all, and that makes me happy. But those women, or ladies, have a very long way to go. Everyone is different when painting the same scene. You and I are both French, and we see things with that as part of what we see. We both could paint the same scene, and both paintings would be very good as well as quite different. The American women saw the trees with their own way of seeing, and of course, they will be different.

"One of the reasons I am the painter that I am is that I see much more than anyone else. Light and color are just part of it. When you get to the Louvre next time, look for three or so paintings of nudes—of Venus maybe. See how different they are. Elbows, texture of cloth—everything. It will help you understand art. At least a bit more."

Jean clapped his hands and said, "Okay, I'll do that. The Louvre is like heaven. Maybe I'll also look at one or both of the ladies so I can compare their elbows. They're going to study with Degas, I believe, and he takes Cassatt there often. They talked about him and meeting Mary Cassatt. Maybe he'll work magic with them."

"Ah, yes. Degas and Cassatt. I sat at the café with him before he went to call on Cassatt for the first time. I could see he had plans in mind. He had a silk hat in his hands. He had one of those infuriating batwing collars. He waltzed off. When Degas came back to the café, he bounced like you do in a polka. He told us she wore a white dress and a bonnet with red flowers. Later, he showed us a self-portrait by Cassatt that had her dressed like he remembered her.

"They've been together a while now, and Cassatt is a decent artist. I should add that they are together as artists, painting together nearly every day when she is in Paris. But nothing more than that. I don't know what he does with whomever but nothing with Cassatt. She comes to the café from time to time and shares her art with us. I even like some of her work. Oh, and speaking of work, I'll give you another canvas. Draw your tree later today. Jean wondered if they were outside on the benches because Monet wanted to emphasize outdoor as the place to do art. Only make it a lot bigger. Come on. Let's go into the studio. I'll set you up, and you can paint it. Draw it first, and then paint it. By the way, you are doing well at training your eyes."

They went into the studio so Jean could start his assignment. There were piles of empty canvases and some boards. Another pile contained paintings. Monet pointed to them and told him not to look at them—but he did later. They were paintings of the cathedral in Rouen.

Monet set a nice-sized canvas on an easel. He pointed to a palette and some paints.

"Are those all the paints you use? It looks like eight or nine colors."

"Just these now. Brown, black, and earth colors are gone. Now I use flake white, vermilion, cadmium yellow, chrome yellow, cobalt blue, French ultramarine, emerald green, viridian green, and madder red. That's all—most of the time. Try to put new paint on the spot on the palette where I had it. You know what I want, I hope."

The painting would be Jean's work for the day. He went outside to look at the sun. Soon the light would be right for him to draw his tree, and then he'd come back into the studio to paint it. Monet was famous for being able to quickly capture the essence of a scene and then paint it with the sketch and his memory of the subject of the painting. He did so at times, even though he preached that one should be at the scene when painting it.

Jean thought back to the time Monet had put down Degas in an argument at a café by saying that if an artist started a painting outside and finished it inside the studio, he was painting what he wanted and not what he saw. *Is that what I am doing?* Most of the time, Monet went back to the scene to finish his paintings. Maybe Jean would try to remember exactly what he saw.

When Jean looked at the Rouen cathedral paintings after Monet left him alone, he noted they had thick layers of richly textured paint. He also saw how Monet interwove the colors with careful subtlety, giving his work on the group of canvases light and color that seemed to shimmer.

Tomorrow Jean would join the others in planting water lilies in a pond on the new property. Monet already had some water lilies, as Jean saw in the studio. He would be busy, as he'd been last time. He also would be looking for a comely young lady, hopefully nearby, as he had last time.

Or so he thought.

Monet came up to him as he started to leave the studio. Monet told him to go somewhere to paint what was on both sides of his tree as well as behind it. He pointed to the sky. "Jean, remember where the sun is. Use a lot of color, and bring enthusiasm to the light. I don't need you as a gardener for about three or four weeks. Garden work now is just digging and digging, so take the painting to Paris after you finish it, and make some money. Maybe you'll get lucky with one of those ladies. Come back, and I'll put you in charge of planting after I tell you what to do."

Then We'll Get Our Taxi

When Luisa and Emille reached the Saint-Lazare station in Paris, they went to a bench to sit and talk. On the train, they had spent their time looking at the countryside and had not brought up the subject of what was next.

"Luisa, what do your parents think about you being here alone in Paris and not in Philadelphia? Mine say they trust me, but I won't be surprised by visits. You know what I mean?"

"Mine trust me too, Emille. Apparently. They trusted me when I went to Bryn Mawr College. I even got to make the trip from home to school alone. If I went to a party, sometimes they checked on me, but I liked the ride home."

They chatted about Mary Cassatt's whole family joining her in Paris and living in a nice apartment. Finally, Luisa acknowledged the unspoken question. "Are we going to get an apartment together? With two bedrooms?" She looked down at her hands.

Emille stood up and turned to face her fellow artist. "We both want to study art, which costs money. Sharing an apartment will save some money. And I think that being roommates obviously will give each of us someone to talk with about art and life in general. We're both from a Philadelphia suburb. We can pretend we're both from Boston." She looked out over Luisa's head as if to see far away. Nothing she saw interested her.

"Emille, before, when I mentioned my cousin from Boston, I didn't tell you that she said she would accept me if I had a full Boston marriage." Luisa stood up and extended her hand, and they shook hands. "Let's get a taxi, go to Montmartre, and find our place. Together."

"Wait," Emille said. "Look at the train. See the smoke coming up out of the engine? See the steam at the sides by the front wheels? I want to get my sketch pad out to see if I can show they are different. They are different. Steam and smoke."

"Our teacher who gave us a failing grade would like that,

Emille. I'll sketch them too. Then we'll get our taxi after gathering our other belongings from the lockers here."

Emile's sketch took a bit longer than Luisa's effort because she added more of the details of the engine. Luisa went for a short walk across the tracks after the train had departed. She came back to Emille and reminded her that she didn't have the subject in front of her anymore and was now painting from memory.

They shared their drawings in the taxi. Both ladies found it pleasant that they could comment on each other's sketches and drawings without being upset about any criticisms. Rather, they accepted the points being made as helpful.

They didn't go directly into Montmartre. They stood at the entrance to the street, looking for someone to give them advice about housing.

Artists lived there to save money, not so much for the atmosphere. The artists made their culture at the cafés along their way to the top. They lived there or had studios in Montmartre because housing cost much less there than in other parts of Paris. It would have been difficult to know at first glance that Montmartre was part of Paris.

The many lanes were muddy, often steep, and dominated by merchants crying out about what they were selling. Plainly dressed women had their children with them, and the children often were noisy.

The top of the road looked like an ordinary French village, which meant almost nothing to the women from Philadelphia. Both ladies had been warned of artists and other men who sought sexual encounters with American women. "Where am I to find a place to sleep?" a woman might ask, only to be told, "With me." Luisa and Emille joked about that imagined dialogue, but both were clear in their own minds about how to behave. Jean had been right when he'd said they were formal ladies who kept everything in their lives proper.

Good Luck with Your Art

T he taxi had dropped them off at the street entrance to Montmartre. After they got out, they looked around and eventually saw an artist with his easel. They walked over to him and looked at his work. "That's nice," Luisa said. "We're hoping to be artists too."

"I wish you luck."

"Sir, can you tell us where we might find an apartment in Montmartre?"

"No, it's too loose and even dangerous. Go a bit that way," he said, pointing, "and you'll find apartment buildings that will be what you want. And good luck with your art."

The ladies began to look for an apartment where he'd pointed. The first one they saw had one bed, though it was wide enough for two adults. At the same moment, they both said, "Too small."

When they walked to the second apartment, they both said, "Too intimate," again at the same time, and laughed. It had two beds with a nightstand between them. They both commented simultaneously that there was no place for the easels, and then they laughed even louder.

The landlord asked what they were laughing at. Emille turned to him and said, "That is the third time we have said the same thing about the same thing, and it's funny because we haven't known each other for that long." He just looked at them. The ladies suspected he thought them to be crazy Americans.

They decided to jointly rent an apartment and save a bit of money. The third place they saw was a large two-bedroom apartment with only a few pieces of furniture. They claimed the space as their studio. The apartment was a short walk from the entrance to Montmartre.

Luisa looked out the window. "This is a second-floor unit. Do you have anything higher?"

"Do you want the penthouse? It's twice the cost per month."

"No, just higher for the light. We are artists, and light helps us. Longer time to work probably."

"I have an apartment like this on the fifth floor. But listen, no parties! If you bring a man up here, or two, that's your decision. But my decision is that there will be no loud noises. No parties. Understood?"

After debating for only a moment, the two ladies agreed on the fifth-floor unit when they saw it, and they signed the lease.

The landlord finally left them alone.

"Which room do you want, Luisa?"

"Let's look," Luisa said, going into one bedroom and then the other. "I can't see a difference. Should we flip a coin?"

"No. Finding a coin might take too long. That room is on the left. This one is on the right. Put out your hand with one or two fingers, with that room being number one. On three. Ready? One. Two. Three," she said, and both revealed two fingers. "I forgot to tell you. Two twos mean you get that one." She pointed to her right. "Let's unpack and find a place for dinner."

They planned to go to the Louvre tomorrow, hoping to find Degas and Cassatt working among the great art. They would bring their equipment along with them, knowing that working there, as Degas did, would greatly improve their skills.

At dinner, the conversation turned to talk about Degas as a person rather than as an art instructor. "Lots of people have told me that Edgar is perfectly proper with Mary Cassatt." Luisa waved her hand at the people eating in the café to indicate she had quoted lots of people.

Emille laughed. "Have you heard from that many people that he's not so proper with other ladies? Or should I say with many women?"

"Well, of course I've heard that. But not from many people. And I don't want to hear it from men. Well, Jean maybe, but I haven't heard that from him. I feel like a man will tell me about what Degas does only so I will consent to doing the same things with him."

The conversation stopped when their main course arrived. After eating, they went back to their new apartment, chatted a bit about Giverny, and then went to bed.

Let's Share One Mailbox

The next morning, as they were leaving the apartment building, the landlord happened to be in the lobby. Luisa asked him where they could find the post office. "We want to write to our parents in Philadelphia and get mail from them, of course."

"Use this building's address to get your mail."

"Not yet. Is the post office near?"

"Just down the street." He pointed and then went into another room.

The ladies walked toward Montmartre. Luisa shook her head. "I don't trust him. I don't want mail to come to the apartment, because he might steal money my parents send, and he would certainly pry into my life. Not that I'm doing anything bad."

"Well, Luisa, let's share one mailbox at the post office."

Both ladies laughed when Emille noted that her mail would be intimately together with her friend's mail and said, "We will have a Boston mailbox."

"Speaking of sharing, we need to stop at that café that has the haystack Monet told us to buy."

"Café de la Nouvelle Athénes."

"Right. It will be good for us to study that haystack after we buy it. I'm going to make notes so when I see another one, maybe I can find the differences. We can put it in our apartment before we go to the Louvre today."

As they entered the café, they both made a quick survey of the customers and smiled when they didn't see any artists gathered together. Luisa began to circle the room with Emille right behind her. They came to a painting of a woman, and they both stared at her breasts, or where they were under the dress the model wore. "This one's by Jean," Luisa whispered.

"I like the high-waisted dress she's wearing. I don't think she's pregnant, but she does have a bust worthy of emphasizing."

Neither lady looked at the other's bust then.

They continued to move along the wall and came to the haystack painting they wanted. "We'll split the cost," Luisa said softly, tapping Emille's left forearm.

As they continued to circle, they came up to Jean's self-portrait. "Good-looking guy," Luisa said. "Does he appeal to you?"

Emille shook her head. "Not my type."

"What is your type?"

"Go buy the Monet. I'll give you your half of the money when you join me at a table. I'll also order some chardonnay to celebrate." Emille went to the table, waved to a waitress to order the wine, and then sat down. She positioned her chair so she could see who came into the café. Because of the late time in the morning, she didn't expect any artists. Her honor still didn't let her feel comfortable with most artists, unless Degas sat with them or if they were properly introduced to her. That thought surprised her, but he showed signs of protecting her and Luisa as well.

Luisa negotiated for the painting, finally telling the bartender that Monet himself had told her to buy it. "So don't keep the price so high." She brought it to the table and put it on a chair where they both could look at it. They raised their glasses of wine to celebrate.

That Explains Your Accent

The waitress came back to their table. "I speak English. Would you like to have lunch? The food is French, and it is amazingly good."

"We speak English too," Luisa said. "We're from Philadelphia."

"That explains your accent. And your American clothing. My English has a French accent. I'm from Paris, and my mother is from New York City." She took out a notepad. "Would you like menus, or can I suggest a great lunch? An appetizer and a nice soufflé."

Emille continued to look at Monet's haystack painting, picking it up to see it up close.

Luisa stared at the waitress. "That sounds like a good lunch. How is your mother doing? Oh, and tell me more about the lunch. We like to have French food as often as we can." She put both of her palms on the table.

"My mother is in Rome. I have a half sister who speaks Italian and English—with an accent, of course. Mother comes to Paris from time to time, only once with my half sister. The appetizer is called *millas*. We boil water and stir in cornmeal. We stir for, oh, fifteen minutes. Then we pour the cornmeal onto a cheesecloth-lined baking sheet, cover it with a wrap, and put it on ice until the cornmeal is firm. Then we cut the millas into thin strips and fry them in butter until they are golden brown. You will truly enjoy them. I will bring another glass of wine if you want also."

"What do you think, Emille?"

They both said yes at the same time and then smiled. Emille put the Monet painting back on the chair and picked up her glass. They made a toast to the millas.

When the waitress went to the kitchen, Emille commented on the New York City woman having children in the fine cities of Europe. "Paris and Rome are better than New York City but maybe not Philadelphia."

Luisa agreed and then said the waitress was pretty. She looked at the Monet haystack.

When the waitress came to the table, Luisa asked her to tell them her name. "First name is all I need. You are a nice person."

"My name," she said as she set the wine in front of them and put the millas on the table, "is Camille. May I tell you about the main course?"

"Of course," Luisa said, smiling. "Tell us."

"It is a spinach soufflé. We sauté the spinach until the juices evaporate. We also cook in some flour—*whisking* is the English word, I think. We put in some milk and whisk to help it thicken. We add the cooked spinach and put in some nutmeg and pepper. Then we put some of the spinach in the egg yolks and put that back in the hot spinach. The egg whites are beaten and added to the spinach. We bake it for, oh, half an hour so it puffs up. I'll bring yours out in a few minutes. Enjoy your millas."

"Thanks, Camille," Luisa said as the waitress walked away. When Camille went behind the bar, she said, "Emille, do you remember that Camille was the name of Monet's first wife?"

"Yes, I do remember." Emille picked up the painting once more. "She had his first child several years before they got married. You saw his son. Jean is his name. Not our Jean. Monet's son was about twelve when his mother died. Of cancer."

Camille brought the soufflé to their table along with another glass of wine. The food smelled delicious and tasted every bit as good, they confirmed. Both ladies were careful to sip the wine, not drinking it too fast.

Dark at Their Table

Luisa and Emille left the café after lunch, mutually agreeing that the walk to the Louvre would moderate the effects of a heavy lunch and three glasses of wine. They laughed when Emille said she felt much more French upon leaving the café. The sun felt warm as they walked, keeping them content yet not inducing the need for a nap. The Louvre had attained much praise for its collection of the masters of art. They hoped its art would energize them too. It would be the first visit for both of them. They were pleased to see that the line of people entering the museum looked shorter than they had been told to expect. They bought tickets and went through the fascinating entry.

When people entered the museum, often, they hurried to see da Vinci's wonderful painting *Mona Lisa*. The museum had acquired *Mona Lisa* from King Francis I about one hundred years ago.

The two ladies almost bumped into each other, as their eyes could not look away from the art. Their agenda for the day simply involved finding and talking with Edgar Degas, who had promised to introduce them to Mary Cassatt. Degas had made the promise yesterday in the café they had just left. Luisa and Emille had chosen to sit far away from the marble-topped tables where some of the impressionists were sitting. Both ladies had felt the need to be introduced to those artists before they sat with them. The darkness at their table had kept Luisa and Emille from seeing what Degas looked like, even though they had taken a short painting lesson from him. The canvases had held their total attention during the lesson.

They wandered through the galleries without seeing him. They saw only aspiring artists sitting on the floor while painting their own copies of the great paintings. After an hour of frustration at their inability to find Degas, Luisa asked a museum guard if he could tell her if and where Degas might be found.

"Do you know Mr. Degas?" he replied. He repressed a yawn and then looked at them.

Emille nodded and said, "Everybody who comes here a lot, like you, must know him. Do you know him?"

The guard knew he needed to keep famous artists from being harassed. "Have you even met Mr. Degas?"

"We met him once—last night in the Café de la Nouvelle Athénes," Emille answered. "Also, we had a partial lesson with him. We're hoping to take more lessons from him, of course."

"Go down this hall to the third gallery. He will be the man in the hat. A new straw hat with a feather."

They thanked him and then rushed off to the gallery, where they saw a man in a straw hat copying or analyzing a painting: *The Holy Family* by Rembrandt. They learned later that the Louvre had acquired it in 1793.

"Should we disturb him?" Emille asked Luisa. "Or should we stand around until he notices us?"

Luisa didn't answer but went to a painting near the entrance and at least pretended to study it. Eventually, Degas noticed them and put down his brush. He stood up and waved for them to come to him. He bowed and waited for each to extend her hand to shake. He thought of the fees for their lessons and smiled.

"Good afternoon, ladies. It is a pleasure to see you again. Did you enjoy your visit to Giverny? Did Mr. Monet treat you pleasantly?" His smile suggested he knew what the answer would be.

"No," Luisa replied, "but we learned some things. Emille had us draw both smoke and steam coming from the locomotive when we got back to the Paris station—to show the difference between them. But when we were there, we didn't see sunlight like he does."

"Did you show him your artwork?"

"I did, but when he rejected it, Emille didn't even take hers out of her bag. You were right, of course."

"Of course. Well now, I want to finish this work," Degas said, pointing to his canvas. "I will be back here tomorrow, and then we can talk. About your lessons."

"Will Mary Cassatt be here?"

"No, she's away, painting a mural for the 1893 World's Columbian Exposition. See you tomorrow. Bring a canvas and your paints so we can get you both started."

They watched Degas resume copying the Rembrandt painting, each guessing privately what Degas would add next. Neither lady guessed right often. When he turned to look at them and frowned, they left, deciding to see more of the museum.

Check on the Ladies

Jean liked the breakfasts at Giverny. He had some great Belgian waffles that morning with a syrup the waitress said came from Monet's maple trees. He also slept well in the boardinghouse with the other gardeners and workers. Last night, he'd finished his painting in the studio with only candles for light. Now he felt anxious to fix it and make it better. In an hour or so, the sunlight would be as it had been when he started the painting.

He took the easel out of the studio, along with the palette and paints he had been using, to finalize the painting. The tree in the center displayed the light as he had captured it on the small canvas when Luisa and Emille were being tested by Monet. The sky had streaks of light and clouds. He liked how he had painted the large white cloud almost hovering above the tree. He saw that he had to fix the bushes and grass on either side of the tree to get the same effect from the sun. He knew he couldn't see well enough with just candlelight to get it right. He stepped back from the canvas and bowed to the squirrel he had added to the base of the tree. The squirrel looked up at the tree, as if deciding to climb up it. It was rare to find a painting by Monet with such an animal, because Monet didn't like what he called gimmicks in his art. Jean wondered what his reaction would be to the critter.

He started to work on the bushes and grass and had just about finished, when Monet came up to him. "Jean, I see you are nearly done." He walked up to the canvas and looked at it from different angles, as he always did. "Ha, I like your squirrel. It's going to climb the tree, isn't the little devil? And your tree is well done. Here I would have a bit more light from the sun," he said, pointing to a branch extending out toward the sun. "And you've just about gotten the bushes and grass fixed. I looked at it earlier when you were at breakfast. Much improved since then."

"Thank you. The painting reflects what you have taught me. I truly appreciate your comments. When it's dry, I'll be going back to Paris like you suggested. By the way, how is the garden work coming? My two friends at breakfast, Georges and Leon, said the work took all their energy. 'Digging and digging' is how they said it."

"They are good workers. Yes, there is a lot of hard digging, but soon I will have my pond, and you can supervise the water lily planting, like we discussed. Have a good time in Paris; sell the painting. And check on the ladies who left here angry with me."

"Claude, they're just too new at artwork to understand. I hope they'll learn what they need. Oh, another question. How is Pierre? Are you teaching him?"

"My starving artist? He went back to Paris after telling me he'd learned so much from me. Of course, he didn't learn much at all. And he proved himself to be unfit to be a gardener. Enjoy Paris. I'll see you when the pond is dug."

He walked off, going to his house's private studio. Jean cleaned up in the studio where he had been working and then went to take the shuttle to the train. At that point, he considered the painting dry enough to travel.

On the ride to Paris, he had a happy thought. Luisa and Emille had said they would buy the painting of the haystack by Monet. When they got to the Café de la Nouvelle Athénes, they would see his two paintings. It would be interesting, to say the least, to see what they thought of them, and he would be interested to see what they thought of his new painting. Monet's opinion mattered much more to Jean, so why was he thinking of the ladies? Then he realized it had nothing to do with the painting. He wanted or even needed to be hugged by them.

During the ride back to Paris, Jean opened the window next to his seat. He sat traveling backward, so the wind didn't directly hit him, and no one sat in the seat behind him. On the route, there were some places where the trees were so close to the tracks that he could touch the branches as he rode along. He smiled at the thought that he was yet another person who loved nature, thanks to Claude Monet.

To Us as Artists

That evening in their apartment, Emille put Monet's haystack painting on an easel in the living room and positioned the bright light of a lamp on the painting. Emille said she wanted to examine it and put her thoughts into words. "See how he uses short, thick strokes of paint? I think the colors were applied, oh, say, side by side so there is simultaneous contrast. See how vivid the colors are?"

"I do see that, Emille. The sky and the land reflect each other. On the train ride back here, I saw some haystacks that had the sun in about the same place that this painting has. For just a moment, I saw the same reflections. But Monet has really captured the light."

"And color," Emille said, "just like we were supposed to do with the trees. He must have put down the wet paint for one color without waiting for the paint of the other colors to dry. See the soft edges and even intermixing of color?"

"You have sharp eyes, Emille. I'll be right back." Luisa went to her bedroom and came back with a bottle wrapped in paper. "Let's celebrate our new knowledge. Get two glasses so we can enjoy this absinthe."

After the drinks were poured and they toasted Monet and his art, they both sat on the couch, facing the painting. As they reached for their glasses on the table in front of them, they came closer to each other. They then moved farther away from each other. They were silent, uncomfortable with the closeness but not able to say so. Emille shut her eyes and ran her hands through her hair.

Finally, Luisa poured more absinthe into both glasses and offered another toast. "To you and to me and to us as artists. Learning about art is a thrill."

Emille smiled, raising her glass to the toasts. "Art has gone from being part of my life to the center, even the essence of my being. I will always toast to us as artists." She looked at the ceiling. "Luisa, am I wrong, or am I seeing art and living here merging? Sort of like I can't seem to separate the two of them. What do you think?"

"I know what you mean, my friend." Luisa sipped her drink.

Emille later refused a third glass of absinthe, saying she felt what she had taken and didn't want to get further influenced by the drink.

"I agree, Emille. Wine at lunch, and now this. I'll cork it and maybe have more tomorrow. Maybe we'll be celebrating our lessons with Degas."

They sat quietly, looking at the painting as well as at each other. After a while, Emille reached for the bottle, poured herself a third glass, and offered the bottle to Luisa, who accepted it.

When she'd finished her drink, Emille got up and hugged herself. "I'm going to bed. Thanks for the absinthe, and thanks for your analysis of Monet's painting. Good night."

Each went to her own bedroom for the night.

The Squirrel Is Not Monet

The evening after Jean arrived in Paris, he walked around a lot. He'd grown up on the edge of Paris and liked city life. Plus, he had also learned to love the countryside, with the trees and fields. The train ride worked fine, but he preferred walking by himself or with someone in the country. He did a lot of that at Giverny, which was where he'd learned to love the simple land.

That evening, he felt thirsty and wanted to catch up on the gossip, so he went to the Café de la Nouvelle Athénes, hoping to get a chair with the artists. He took his time, stopping to talk with several artists still outside painting. When he walked into the café, right away, he noticed that Monet's haystack painting had been taken down. *Claude will like to hear that,* he thought. He saw that his friends Camille Pissarro, Edgar Degas, Pierre-Auguste Renoir, Alfred Sisley, and Paul Cézanne had gathered around four marble-topped tables pulled together. Happily, Jean took a vacant chair that happened to position him with his back to his paintings.

After the hellos and teasing remarks, Cézanne asked, "Why are your paintings hanging here in this café?"

"Because they're so good."

"With Monet, I could accept that. He is good. But yours are not that good by any means."

"Relax, Paul," Pissarro said. "Actually, Jean won a card game here. The owner had us play cards and said the winner could hang two of his paintings in the café, where Jean's paintings are now. For a year, I think."

"Two years, Camille. And they had to have been selected to be shown at the Salon first. And my two fit the requirement."

Cézanne didn't look convinced. "Who played in the card game?"

"Pissarro, Sisley, Degas here, and two or three others. Playing cards is not like painting. There is luck involved, and I had some nice surprises in the cards I got."

"Looks like you got lucky with your paintings," Degas said, and then he changed the subject. "How did your time in Giverny go? You get along with Monet, I hear."

"Yes, we get along. For two reasons, I think. One is that I'm a gardener he trusts and approves of. I'm going back in a short while to plant water lilies. And second, he likes that I learn what he teaches me. I have a painting I did there." Jean took the canvas out of his bag and put it on one of the tables so it could lean against the wall.

They all looked at it. Degas said, "The tree stands out. Just like his do. The bushes and grass are in his style too. But the squirrel is not Monet."

"He even liked that. When I'm there to work in the garden, I stay at an apartment for artists and gardeners. This time, I stayed with a friend I made two years ago. He has a room that faces west. At night, when I look out the window, I see nothing, though I know there are a lot of trees out there. In the morning, as the sun continues to rise, slowly, the trees come alive with sunlight on the branches, with shadows on the back side of the limbs, and one branch casts its shadow on a nearby tree. The sun also converts the black or white trees into colors. A black tree has a redness on its highest limbs and branches—not like a fire but like a red blanket. A white poplar turns almost yellow."

"So even Monet's land does what he wants it to," Degas said. "Get the waitress, and we'll drink to your painting. By the way, the waitress said the Philadelphia ladies bought Monet's haystack, so there's room for this one."

Jean thanked him, put his painting back in his bag, and then said that Monet had told the ladies to buy the haystack painting. They'd told Claude they would share the cost and the painting.

Jean enjoyed the toast when the drinks came.

This Will Work Out Best for Me

Back in Giverny, Monet supervised the gardeners who were digging the pond and getting ready to connect the pond to a small brook, the Ru, which was a diversion of the Epte, a tributary of the Seine River. Peasant neighbors were opposed to the project, but Monet went ahead anyway.

Monet continued to mourn the death of his first wife, Camille, though it had been almost fourteen years since she'd died of tuberculosis in 1879. He had made a study in oils of his dying wife on her deathbed. Many years later, Monet would confess that his need to analyze colors had become both the joy and the torment of his life. He said, "I one day found myself looking at my beloved wife's dead face and just systematically noting the colors according to an automatic reflex! The painting showed a terrible intensity of loss, which overwhelmed her features." Monet kept the painting and spent time with it often—actually, it was his only painting he spent any time with—to honor his wife's life.

Those who knew Monet felt that time had begun healing his bereavement. His maid and, later, wife, Alice Hoschedé, helped him raise his two sons. She took them to Paris to live alongside her own six children. In time, Monet found Giverny and first rented and then bought the house, the surrounding buildings, and the land for his gardens. The house sat near the main road between the towns of Vernon and Gasny at Giverny. The property included a barn that doubled as a painting studio, plus orchards and a small garden. Only a few blocks separated the house from the local schools the children attended, and the surrounding landscape offered many suitable motifs for Monet's work. Beginning in 1890, Monet built a greenhouse and a second studio, a spacious building brightly lit with skylights.

In 1893, Monet went out every day to the pond to inspect the work of the gardeners and give them their assignments for the day. Leon Duret, the gardener who had become a friend of Jean's and often relaxed with him with a bottle of wine, became the lead gardener. "You will be my gardener, Leon," Monet said, "until Jean returns. I know you and he are friends, so this will work out best for me."

"Mr. Monet, yes, we are friends, and it will work out best for us as well."

Monet waved his hand at his gardeners and went to the studio. The other gardeners had heard what Monet said and understood that Leon had his ear. They resumed working as Monet walked away.

Monet resumed working on one of his paintings of the cathedral in Rouen. People had liked the first few paintings, and he had the opportunity to raise the price on his later canvases. Alice called to Monet when lunch had been put on the dining table. She'd had the cook reheat the boeuf bourguignon from last night's dinner. Alice met him in the yellow dining room and sat at his right side. She had a glass of red wine, while Monet had a glass of plum brandy.

"One of our neighbors, obviously a peasant, spoke to me when I spent time in the garden near the road. She said that many who live near the brook are unhappy about what you are doing to it," Alice said.

"Who cares?"

"I just thought maybe you could explain to them that what you are doing is harmless. If it is." Alice served him first and then herself.

"They'll see it is harmless in time. And I guarantee you they will not appreciate the beauty of the gardens I am going to produce. All they care about is harmlessness. Not beauty."

"Why not?" Alice asked before sipping her wine.

"Because they would have had gardens before we moved here if they had any sense of beauty. But they don't. Tell dear Marguerite this is delightful beef." He finished his portion, got up, and went to resume his painting.

Alice Watched for a Minute

When he returned from Rouen, Monet parked the steam car and then went to his studio, where he had given Jean the canvas for his tree painting. He briefly glanced at the stack of paintings; every one was of the Rouen cathedral. He had decided the variety of light and color showed how visual sensations changed because of changing sunlight, even though the cathedral itself did not physically change its structure from one canvas to the next. He put the most recent canvas on the easel and started to paint.

Alice came into the studio and walked up to the painting of the Rouen cathedral on the easel. "Why is the paint so thick? Can't you paint it just like it is?"

"How many times, Alice, do I have to tell you that the texture from the paint lets me show the effect of sunlight at certain specific times of day? I've had nightmares about this building and all the possible colors. I have to come back after a number of days to each painting because I find something I did not see the day before."

He took off his hat and rubbed his head, scratching at the spot where his sideburns ended at a bald spot. "That's where I went earlier this morning. Here I'm showing the progression of shadows in the entrances to the building. Yellow, blue, and brown all have a role in showing some part of the whole. This thick paint, called impasto, is what I use to show the architectural aspects of the church. I mean cathedral. And look at the sky. See how the blue darkens just a bit from right to left? See how the shorter center part casts shadows on the taller part to the left? This morning, I met the priest at the cathedral. He came to see me and left after a brief conversation. The park behind the studio is full of benches because the members want, or need, to talk to each other. He also said the church is where one talks to God."

"Relax, Claude. But keep talking. When you describe what you are doing like you just did and why you are doing it, I understand the painting much better. I wish I could see the actual cathedral and maybe go to Mass. I see what you see in the painting itself. The change in the sky is so very slight."

"It is what I saw. I have good eyes, and that is what I saw."

"You have such a beautiful way of showing what you see. Oh, and do you think I—or we—could go to Mass at the cathedral?"

"I don't do Mass. You know that. I told the priest that too. If I show up, that would make me a liar. Of course, you could go to Mass while I paint." Monet picked up a tube of blue paint, squeezed more onto his palette, and began applying it to the main entrance as a shadow above a brown lower shadow. "Anyway, Alice dear, when I need to paint the cathedral in the morning, I'll take you along, and you can go to Mass and sit on a bench in the park. You can talk to the priest if you want."

Alice watched for a minute and then silently left so as not to disturb him. As she walked back to the house, she realized she needed to spend a lot more time watching him paint. She felt the opportunity for learning gave her much that she hadn't even imagined possible. And she did want to talk to the priest.

His undisturbed time to paint did not last long. Gardener Leon Duret came into the studio, holding the gloves he had just taken off his hands. He knocked on a post and then coughed. Monet ignored him, so Leon walked up to the artist. "Sir, you said I am your gardener. I have a major question."

"Can't it wait? Can't you see I'm doing something?" Monet waved him away.

"Sir, the work we are doing will have to stop until you answer my question. What should we do with a beautiful wisteria tree that is in the path of our digging? Do we cut it down? Or go around it, which will endanger it unless we go far around it?"

"I don't remember a wisteria tree. Are you sure you are on the path I told you to use so the water flows directly into the pond?"

"Yes, sir."

"Well, damn it, I will go look at this mystery tree. But you'd better be right."

Leon stayed a few steps behind Monet, hoping to avoid a lecture on the walk to the path. When they got there, Monet took one look and then walked back to his studio. As he left, he said, "Okay, Leon. You're right. The tree goes."

Instead of going into the studio, Monet sat on the green bench by the front door of his house, looking at the row of nasturtiums of the same color on the other side of the walk. Some plants were a bit overgrown, and he added pruning them to his mental list of gardener assignments. As he sat there, Alice walked up carrying a bag with something in it.

She sat on the same bench. "Claude, I met that peasant lady today over by our border when I went looking for some mushrooms." She lifted her bag. "Her name is Felise."

"What kind of name is that?"

"It is from medieval French, she said. She has had some schooling, but her parents did not. I suspect the family has lived there for centuries. I almost laughed out loud. She kept looking past me, as if she wanted to find you. Or see you."

"She might have been wanting to see a famous painter or to complain about the pond, but I don't have any idea who she might or could be, Alice. No, not to my knowledge."

"Claude, let's go to bed. Now."

"Alice, it's the middle of the afternoon. What do you mean?"

"It would be nice to have an afternoon delight." Alice didn't hint that she suspected he had been having a relationship with the peasant woman and had just come back from such an affair. *If he can't do it, it's because he just did it.*

Monet stood up, kissed Alice on the forehead, and told her he needed to go to the canvas on the easel he'd set up in the studio to work on when the sun was right, and the time had arrived finally.

We Haven't Painted Together Yet

Luisa and Emille went to the Louvre the next morning, each bringing a canvas and some paints. The sun shone brightly, and they both felt the heat and enjoyed the feeling of being warmed. They were stopped at the entrance by a guard. "Do you ladies have a permit to paint here?"

"No, sir," Luisa said. "We are to meet Mr. Degas for our lessons with him. Is he here yet? He has a student before us today but had no student as he painted alone yesterday."

"Lessons with Degas? Did you talk with him recently?"

"Yesterday," Emille answered. "Here in a studio down that way."

"Well, he is in the same gallery as yesterday. You may go to him, and I will stop by to be sure what you have said is true. The museum does not like people to make copies of our fine works just to sell cheaply. Legitimate students of known artists are, of course, permitted."

"Luisa, are we legitimate?" Emille said.

Luisa didn't answer; she just laughed, as did the guard. The ladies curtsied and went to the gallery. When they arrived, Degas sat relaxing while another student packed up her canvas and supplies.

"Good morning, ladies. How nice that you are on time. Set up this second easel so you each have one facing the painting I worked on yesterday: Rembrandt's *The Holy Family*." He waved to his student who had finished packing her equipment. She affirmed that she would be back tomorrow at the same time.

"Are we to copy this, sir?" Emille asked.

Degas walked over to the painting, blocking their view of it. "Not yet. And please call me Edgar. There is no need to be so formal. Tell me first—how do you start a painting? What goes on the canvas first? How much do you think about what you intend to paint?"

Emille pointed to Luisa to answer first.

Luisa stepped back from her canvas and replied, "I can only speak for myself, because we've never painted together. We've seen each other's art but only after the paint is dry. I myself sit and watch my subject, looking at it from different angles. I don't worry about where the sun is, as Mr. Monet does, though maybe I should. When I'm ready to start, I put my brush where I think the center will be. I like to work outward." Luisa went back to her canvas, putting down her brush. She nodded to Emille.

"Luisa is right; we haven't painted together yet, though our apartment will give us that opportunity. We're on the fifth floor and have big windows. But to answer your questions, Edgar, it depends on my subject. If I'm painting a landscape, I pick the most prominent feature and start there. If I'm painting a portrait, I lightly sketch a square or rectangle to fit the person, whether seated or standing. Then I put the person's head in and go from there."

Degas looked from one lady to the other several times. "Fine. Soon you can start your paintings, but before you do, I want to tell you something. I know you have been to see Monet. Did you see him start a painting?"

The ladies shook their heads. The painting they'd seen him work on had been started the day before they saw it.

"Once in front of his easel, he draws in a few lines with the charcoal, and then he attacks the painting directly, handling his long brushes with an astounding agility and an unerring sense of design. He paints with a full brush and uses four or five pure colors; he juxtaposes or superimposes the unmixed paints on the canvas. His landscape is swiftly set down and could, if necessary, be considered complete after only one session, a session that lasts only while the effect he is seeking lasts, sometimes an hour and often much less. He is quite conscious of where the sun is."

Degas looked the ladies in their eyes to be sure they understood what he told them. "Monet almost always works on two or three canvases each time he goes out to the location of the subject he is painting. He brings them all along and puts each on the easel as the light changes to suit that painting. This is his method. It is not my method, and I'll share mine with you at another time. Now, go ahead. Start the painting your way. I'll come back in one hour to see how you are doing."

7

I Like to Imagine She
Is Looking at Me

Luisa and Emille did not know that when Degas walked out of their gallery, he ran into Jean in another gallery. He told Jean where they were but said not to disturb the ladies. He explained that he had them copying a Rembrandt painting, and Jean would most likely distract them. Jean made him promise he'd suggest they come to the café that night. He felt they were more likely to accept such an invitation from Degas than from him.

Degas had no problem with doing that. "Jean, I might have thought of that without your prompting. They have a long way to go to be good at art, but they both have the enthusiasm and ambition to paint well, so sitting with the group of our artists will expose them to greatness and give them a goal to aim for. And what about you? Are you a good artist? If so, how good?"

Jean closed his eyes and rubbed his forehead with his hands. "I'm picturing the art I've created. I think it is good, but none of them is a masterpiece. Your works of art and those of Monet, Cézanne, and the others are clearly masterpieces. Mine are not. Yet. That's why I need to talk to you about painting."

"You paint outside. You're Monet's student. You don't need or want what I teach. You're just coming around to see me so you can see the Philadelphia ladies." Degas pretended to wash his hands, intending for Jean to get the point.

"Do you remember my paintings at the café?"

"You painted those indoors."

"Yes, but they would look the same if I had painted them outside. There is no background. Both portraits are in an invisible setting."

"Have you ever seen a portrait painted outdoors?"

"I'm not sure what I want to paint. Monet knows. You know, you two are different, but you are both happy."

"We both know what we like to paint."

"Sure. But I don't yet know what would make me happy."

"Try my nudes," Degas said.

"Thanks. You know I have some paintings you helped me with. Why don't you believe me? Forget about me and those ladies. They are your students. Just for the fun of it, however, tell me—which one is the better artist?"

Degas declined to tell him which of the two ladies from Philadelphia would eventually be the better artist.

"I know, Edgar, that it isn't easy to compare artists until they fully mature. As artists, I mean. I see them both being mature as women."

"You do? What are your intentions, Jean?"

"At this point in their lives, both ladies are truly committed to being artists. That, as you know better than I, takes so much of what we have that we don't have time for anything else. Has Mary Cassatt any time for a social life?"

"Leave Mary out of this." He stood, looking at a painting. "Yes, she is committed to her art and totally uncommitted to anything else."

Jean walked over to the painting, which showed a woman sitting on large rocks arranged to make a chair. She wore a gray dress with a neckline at her shoulders, showing the tops of her breasts. He had seen it before, of course, and liked it. The frame said the painting had been done by Pierre-Paul Prud'hon back in 1823. "Edgar, did you know this artist?"

Degas looked at the lettering. "No. Manet is the only one of us old enough to have met him. I do like the lady, which is why I'm here while those ladies are working on their paintings. Especially I like how she is looking away to something we can't see. I like to imagine she is looking at me."

Both artists looked at the painting from different angles. Finally, Jean said, "Do you imagine she is Mary?"

"I said leave her out of this. Go somewhere. Anywhere. I'll tell the ladies to come to the café tonight. You can try whatever you have in mind."

Jean waved to Degas and walked out the main entrance. He always enjoyed the steps and statues, many of which were life-sized and, in some cases, doing things they shouldn't have been doing as openly as they were. But white marble had a different code of living than people did. The view of outside was also a delight. The sky had cleared of clouds, and bright sunlight bathed him and the museum.

Jean walked back to his studio in Montmartre, weighing in his mind which of the two ladies he might prefer. Degas had implied they were different in their perspectives about art. Would their art help him to decide? Would their responses to him and his art open a door for him to approach at least one of them? Jean shook his head, wondering if they were a waste of his time. Not a waste, he decided, because wondering what the ladies would do gave him pleasure.

Take What the Other Has Done as Your Focus

Luisa and Emille began painting as soon as Degas left. They quickly lost awareness of each other as they focused on their own canvases. Emille paused every ten minutes or so to step back, look at her canvas, and then go to Rembrandt's painting to compare what she had done in detail with Rembrandt's art. Luisa paused only for a few seconds occasionally and then went right back to her painting.

The Rembrandt painting showed Mary holding baby Jesus as she nursed him. His crib was at her feet. An open window let sunlight into the room, and it shone brightly on Jesus and on the back of a person standing by the window, presumably Joseph, if only because of the title. He was part of the holy family. "Perhaps," Emille said, "this painting includes Joseph for that reason." The floor was made of planks of wood, with the sunlight on part of the wood. The artwork affirmed Rembrandt's skill and also raised the question of what he thought about the virgin birth, because Joseph stood by. Neither lady could be certain what Rembrandt thought, though Emille said she wanted to talk about that at dinner.

Emille's painting started with Mary, and then she added Jesus nursing on her lap. Luisa's painting started with Jesus in the sunlight and then focused on the window as the source of the sunlight. She sketched in the planks of the floor to make sure the sunlight came in a straight line. There were so many details that neither lady came close to making a full copy. They each chose different details.

Degas came back to them, clapping his hands as he walked up to them. He asked them to stand back so he could see their efforts. Emille made a sniffing sign with her nose, implying that Degas had been drinking. Luisa nodded in agreement.

"Luisa," Degas said, "you seem fascinated by the light. You even started sketching it outside the window. Has Monet influenced you that much?"

Luisa laughed. "I didn't even think of him or his fixation on light and color. It just struck me as Rembrandt's way of showing Jesus as superior to the rest of them. He is God, of course."

"Of course, Luisa. Can you tell what time of day it is from the angle of the light?"

"Not exactly, Edgar. But I think it is midday, which would be a time to feed Jesus as well. Women know that."

Degas turned to look at Emille's work. "You have made a loving effort to show Jesus and Mary as being the center of the painting, not only in placement but also in importance. Very nice. You also have the crib where it is on Rembrandt's painting. You are focused on the people, Jesus as God. Your painting is more spiritual or religious. That's neither good nor bad, but it shows how you found your perspective."

Emille turned to look at Luisa. Before she could say anything, Degas spoke again. "I am not judging one painting over the other. Both are good efforts with a truly complicated painting. I would like you both to continue working on your paintings for a while, and then come back here tomorrow. Okay?"

The ladies quickly agreed to return.

"I have a thought. Luisa focused on the light, and Emille focused on the mother and child. Each of you should continue your work but take what the other has done as your focus. I'll see you tomorrow, unless I see you tonight at the Café de la Nouvelle Athénes. You would be invited to join us at our group of tables. Some well-known artists will be there. Please do consider joining me at the tables."

The ladies went back to their work after spending some time looking at each other's painting. Luisa nodded as if she understood what Degas wanted her to do. Emille went back up to the Rembrandt painting before starting her work. Emille also said that going to the café sounded like a good idea. Neither of them mentioned Jean.

What Each of Us Would Exhibit

Jean stood looking in the window of a shop across the street from Café de la Nouvelle Athénes, waiting for Luisa and Emille to show up. If he sat at the table with the other artists, the women might not join the group, he thought. In time, the ladies arrived, each holding a green parasol, which went nicely with Emille's white dress and not as nicely with Luisa's blue outfit. They went into the café, and he waited long enough to expect they had been seated with the artists.

When he went inside, Luisa was standing in front of his painting of the woman that focused on her breasts, while Emille stood in front of his self-portrait. They both turned and went to the marble tables to sit on either side of Degas. He waved for Jean to take a seat at the other end of the group of tables. Jean went to that seat, patting several of the artists on their shoulders.

Luisa waved to him and said she liked his painting of the woman. Emille smiled and said she had no comment on his portrait. Luisa looked at the drink Degas had in front of him. Degas saw her looking, so he picked it up for a sip. "This is absinthe. The green absinthe is poured over ice. Cold water is then poured over a sugar cube to soften the bitter taste of the wormwood in the absinthe. This drink, with the water and sugar, is now a pale, luminous yellow liquid. Try one."

A waiter brought them each a glass of absinthe and then came to Jean for his order. "Red wine. Syrah," Jean told him.

Cézanne coughed to get their attention and said they should be talking about how they could improve the art display they planned to present. "It is only six weeks away." Everyone looked at Jean.

"My two paintings back there," Jean said, pointing to them, "will be at the event if they aren't sold, as will the one I showed some of you."

"Your tree with the squirrel?" Degas asked.

"Of course." Jean thanked the waiter and took a sip of the Syrah he'd brought to him.

Emille wanted to know if they were referring to the painting Jean had done at Giverny, and he started to tell her what it was and when he'd painted it, when Cézanne coughed again and asked that they all give a bit of a report on what each would exhibit. They went around the tables. Paul Cézanne started the reports, and Alfred Sisley went second. They listed their choices, as did all the others at the tables. When it came to Luisa, Degas simply raised his hand in her direction and then told what he would bring. "You ladies are a few years away from an event like this."

The women both ordered another absinthe.

Cézanne complained that the Salon had hung his painting so high on the wall that no one could see it. The group promised not to do that to him this time. Paul took the teasing without reacting, which surprised them. To a follower of the impressionist movement, the paintings the artists listed would make a wonderful show. Jean said so, feeling good that he would be included.

As time wore on, Luisa and Emille were finishing their fourth absinthe, when Edgar stood up and offered his arms to the two ladies sitting next to him. When they stood up, he stepped back, and the ladies almost fell into a hug. They both tried to sit back down, but he held them by their upper arms. "You are my students, and I want you to function tomorrow at your lesson. I will walk you home."

Neither woman could argue with him, if they even understood what he said to them.

The artists all stood up, as gentlemen were to do, and watched them walk out of the café. Each held on to one of Degas's arms, clearly wobbling. After they left, Cézanne said, "I'm going to tell Degas not to invite them to come here again. They will have to produce a decent painting before they are welcome, at least as long as I am here."

Several artists disagreed with him. Cézanne stood up. "Maybe I'm being too strict. Everyone here has done the same thing at least several times, including me. The ladies want to be artists, and being at these tables has been part of all our paths to greatness. So instead, I'll ask Degas if they are making progress. That will be how I decide what I say." He sat back in his chair and said he was done talking, leaving the artists to do their things. Jean had another Syrah.

Jean, How Do You Know Pierre?

To Jean's surprise, one of two men who'd just entered the café shouted his name. "Jean! Jean! It's Pierre Stéphane. Remember me?"

Jean turned to look. He recognized Pierre from the train to Giverny and the disastrous art lesson with Monet and the two ladies. The other man with Pierre looked more familiar to Jean. Novelist Émile Zola regularly sat with the artists at the tables in the café.

Pierre shook Jean's hand, put his hand on Jean's arm, and looked as if he planned to hug Jean. "I'm a novelist now, Jean. My painting took so long to go anywhere, and here I am. My first novel will be published soon, thanks to Émile. Plus, I've written some articles for some publications—on French naturalism, which is how I met Émile. He found a publisher for me. We just left that place. I'm so excited."

Degas stood up to greet Pierre. "Jean, how do you know Pierre?"

Jean sipped his wine as he thought about his answer. "I met Pierre on a train to Giverny. When we were there, I didn't have much time for us to talk. He wanted to know about Mr. Monet, and I replied that I didn't know Pierre so didn't feel I could introduce him to the artist."

"That's right, Jean. Edgar, Jean did the best he could, and Mr. Monet even gave me a great dinner. I went to one lesson with him and with two ladies who had no time for me. But I left happy with my experiences there. That's really when I realized I would be better off as a novelist. Jean, I will get you a copy of my novel."

Zola told Pierre to stop talking several times, as he felt that what the artists had to say overwhelmed what, if anything, Pierre had to say. Jean learned that Pierre didn't fully agree with Zola on the question of miracles at Lourdes so Jean quietly said he would like to talk with him when the café conversations ended.

Pierre drank some absinthe—a bit quickly, Jean thought. Jean relaxed and sipped his wine, happy to hear the artists bragging about their paintings. Sometimes an artist would say something that Jean thought he could use. Cézanne went into great detail about how his efforts to paint the portraits of Provençal men caused him to learn some new words to have them sit just the way he wanted for the paintings.

Zola watched Pierre try to order yet another absinthe, but his words didn't make sense. Zola stood up, waved the waitress away, and pulled Pierre out of his chair. They left without walking a straight line.

Why Do You Have to Decide?

Eventually, the artists had had enough talk and absinthe. As the group broke up, Cézanne waved Jean over to him and took him aside to a table distant from the group. "How are you doing? Your portraits are both nice, and so is your tree. You do both inside and outside."

"Paul, I've had lessons from Degas and Monet. So far, I haven't decided which will be the one for me." He swirled the small amount of wine in his glass and then drank it.

"Why do you have to decide? You do both quite nicely. Years ago, I worked with Monet. He insisted on en plein air. As I developed my art, I found I like painting inside—not because it's better or whatever. What I choose to paint is more important than where I paint it. As I told you, I'm painting some men playing cards. Provençal men. They belong inside when they play cards. Same with still-life paintings. So you can see that what I paint determines where I am when I paint it."

"Paul, that is helpful. Degas paints ballet dancers or nudes, Monet paints gardens and hay bales, and so on. I still have a problem because I don't know what, if anything, will be my focus. Maybe I will turn out like you, doing both."

Cézanne stood up, patted Jean on his back, and tipped his hat. "I hope I've helped you. I hope you soon find your focus."

Blame It on Absinthe

Degas walked with Luisa and Emille to their apartment, helping them by having them hold on to his arms. On the third try, they found the right building. Degas had to hold the door to the building so each lady could enter separately, as going through the door together would likely have caused them to collide. Climbing the stairs to the apartment on the fifth floor had Degas puffing from the effort as he continued to support both ladies. Luisa took a while but finally found her key and opened the door. Degas said good night and left them to their own abilities in their apartment. Neither appeared to be even slightly functional, but both of them staggered inside.

Degas shut the door. He felt exhausted and went home instead of back to the café. He didn't need any more absinthe, though he considered himself to be functional.

The ladies wandered around their apartment. Luisa tried to find something to eat and then sat on the couch with an apple. Emille went to bed, going to the wrong room. When she decided to go to bed, Luisa found Emille in her bed. Her dress was on the floor.

"I'm confused. I'm so sorry, Luisa. I will try to find my bed." Emille struggled to sit up and then lay down on her back once again.

"Emille, you don't need to move. Get some sleep so we can be artists again tomorrow. That's who we really are."

"Then you use my bed. It's somewhere." She pointed in the direction of outside.

"This is fine. There is lots of room for both of us." Luisa climbed into bed with Emille. They both went to sleep almost instantly.

Hours later, when Luisa turned over in the bed, she saw Emille and moved to hug her as she slept. Luisa went back to sleep. Later, Emille woke, felt Luisa's hug, saw her smile, and didn't do anything to move her. She also went back to sleep with a smile.

In the morning, Emille woke up before Luisa. She gently moved Luisa back on the bed, undoing the hug. Luisa woke up then, and both ladies looked at the ceiling, saying nothing. Emille got out of the bed, picked up her dress, and went to her room. They both began their morning routines, getting ready to go to the Louvre for their lesson. Neither lady said anything as they got ready.

They went to breakfast at the local café, as usual, and finally talked about sleeping in the same bed. "Luisa, I'm so sorry," Emille said. "I became confused. Absinthe is not good for me. I didn't mean anything by sleeping in your bed. Please forgive me."

"What's to forgive? We slept, and now we're rested and ready for Degas."

"Well, I'm going to switch to wine. Probably red wine."

"Emille, are you going to share a bottle with Jean? Just teasing you. The two of us will share the bottle of wine. I too had too much absinthe, which is probably why I hugged you. I don't know. That's the first time in my adult life I've shared a bed with anyone. Now you can forgive me."

"Let's just say that absinthe is out of our lives, and as long as we are asking for forgiveness, what do we say to Degas? Did he come into our apartment?"

"I don't think so. If I remember correctly, he puffed very hard after getting us up the stairs. I think we should not say a thing. If he brings it up, we'll just blame it on absinthe. We don't have it in Philadelphia."

Both ladies hoped Degas would say nothing, and both suspected he would use their embarrassment for something he wanted.

Anyone Who Isn't Family

As they walked from their apartment to the Louvre, Luisa asked Emille if she ever had drunk too much at a party. "I did once, and my parents grounded me for a month. My father's father, Grandfather Slagle, drank too much all the time, which made my father very strict about my use of alcohol," Luisa said.

"Not at a party, but I did once at home with my father. I think he did that to show me what not to do. I felt safe in our home, and Mother refrained from drinking. She put me to bed." Emille laughed. "She didn't sleep with me."

"Let's forget that. Don't bring it up again."

When they arrived at the Louvre, carrying their canvases, they talked to the guard for a moment to catch their breath, though neither Emille nor Luisa admitted to being tired. They learned that Degas had not yet arrived. Then they went to the gallery, where they set up and began working on their paintings.

Emille stood at the Rembrandt for maybe five minutes, trying to see how the light went straight through the window to the floor. She worked to put her mother and child more in line with the light from the window. She spent more time looking at the Rembrandt and her painting than putting paint on the canvas.

Luisa had the angle of the sunlight correctly placed since she'd focused on that aspect when she first started her canvas. She had no trouble placing mother and child in the right place, affirming to herself that her technique worked best.

Degas arrived before Emille finished her realignment of the light. "Well, ladies, I see you have recovered from last night." He smiled. "I also see that you have been hard at work. The guard told me what time you got here. Let me see your work." Degas walked over to Luisa's canvas. "You have made a lot of progress."

"Yes, Edgar. I had the light just right, so all I really had to do was place the mother and child. And the other items in the painting. My approach worked."

"You should always hope your approach works. The approach will not be the same in every case. I should tell you both that my approach—which you might have noticed, since you both saw my work—let me paint the light only in part and then place the mother and child. Good work."

He went to Emille's painting. "Clearly you had some problems. Your initial drawing of the mother and child shows them as they are in Rembrandt's painting. Very well done. The problems started when you placed the window and the light at a different point than Rembrandt. Monet must have told you that light goes in a straight line. Still, you're fixing that. The other problem I see is that the mother and child are so very well done, and the other items in the painting look like afterthoughts. I'm proud of both of you."

"Thank you, sir," they both said. Luisa added that she'd enjoyed the project, and Emille nodded in agreement. Then both stood silently.

"Have you wondered what will come next? Well, of course you have. Today I will let you finish this project here. Tomorrow we will do some things at a studio. I don't know for sure which one yet, so come to the café tonight, and I'll tell you then."

"We didn't exactly make a good impression last night, sir," Luisa said.

Emille walked back to the Rembrandt as Luisa spoke.

"Ah, yes. Last night. Well, last night you held on to my arms so you could get home. Now, today, I am wondering which one of you will be the first to hug me as a thank-you for last night."

Luisa said, "We are from Philadelphia—actually, two very proud suburbs—and we don't hug anyone who isn't family. Well, almost no one. One can hug a gentleman friend if he has been properly introduced to her and if there are family members present to make sure it is proper. I cannot hug you."

Emille went over to them and said, "Mr. Degas, I also cannot hug you. You are my instructor, and I must keep a certain proper course of action between us, starting with keeping our distance. Thank you for your help last night. Both of us are very grateful for what you did. And how you did it. You are a gentleman. Thank you, but we may not hug you. I look forward to seeing you at the café tonight."

Degas waited until both ladies had turned toward their canvases, and then he walked up to them and patted each on her shoulder. Both Emille and Luisa shuddered. Seeing no positive reaction, he left without saying goodbye. They continued to work on their paintings for more than an hour and then packed up and went home, where each took a nap in her own bed.

Anxious to Get Back to a Canvas

Midmorning the next day, Jean took his painting of the tree in Giverny to the open parkland near the Louvre and set it up on a bench so those passing by would see it. He felt that his promise to have it at the showing Cézanne and the other artists were planning only counted on his being in Paris at the time. He expected to be back in Giverny, doing the garden work, so he decided to test the market for his painting. Besides, Monet had been right that Jean could use the money if it sold.

People walked by, going to and coming from the Louvre and other places. The sun felt good without overheating those who walked fast. Many passersby stopped to look at his tree painting, and many laughed at the squirrel. Several people asked if Monet had painted the painting. They recognized the brushstrokes and the effect of light on the tree. He told them Mr. Monet had had him paint it as an exercise at his home and studio in Giverny. "I am the artist," he said.

One gentleman tried to get him to say Monet had created the painting, seemingly knowing that the great artist had not put any paint on the canvas. Jean told him, "I'm proud of my work, and I don't believe in being dishonest. I sense that if you were to buy this painting, which you won't, you would misrepresent it as being by Monet."

The man said something Jean couldn't hear and didn't want to and then walked away.

Jean started to get hungry and had in mind a nice sidewalk café just across the Seine River. Before he could take the painting down, a man in a gray suit and hat came up and asked his price after just glancing at the canvas. When Jean told him, the man took out his wallet and gave Jean the seventy francs he wanted. He bent down to see if Jean had signed the painting, which he had, and he tipped his hat and then walked off with the canvas.

Jean put the money in his pocket and walked toward the Seine and his lunch. After he'd sat at a table and relaxed, he ordered a glass of burgundy and looked at the menu. He chose the herbed goat cheese and tomato tart. He felt good after making his first painting sale and was anxious to get back to a canvas.

When he'd finished his delicious lunch, having resisted a second glass of burgundy to celebrate the sale, he walked slowly to Montmartre, to his studio. On his strolling, he tried to find something he could paint. The portrait of the woman and the self-portrait had been done indoors, as were most portraits. The tree canvas he'd just sold had the tree as the central feature. He thought of Monet's paintings of the Rouen cathedral and then of his hay bales. Monet could handle big and small with equal excellence. Jean continued to wonder what, if anything, he could handle.

Jean thought about the time he'd come upon a large block of trees with the sun behind him. A few branches had had sunlight on them, turning them almost orange in color. As his eyes had followed a branch down out of the sunlight, it had become black. Above that branch had been two areas where the branches and leaves formed what looked like caves of black. One cave had had some spaces at the back that let the blue sky behind the trees show. The other one had shown only black. He also remembered not wanting to paint the trees, even though Monet would have told him to do so.

Along his walk, Jean saw several lovely women; some were offering themselves for sale, and others were selling food and other stuff. He could find a woman to paint, he thought, as he had in the past several times. Unfortunately, none of those efforts had turned into a decent painting. With that thought, he decided to find Degas to learn why he couldn't do justice to female models. He also hoped Degas would help him find another subject for multiple paintings. He would hear arguments for painting inside. Plus, he knew he needed more instructions.

On his walk, once again, he heard his name called out. He turned to see Pierre swinging his arms as he hurried to catch up with him.

Pierre again acted as if he would hug Jean, grabbing his arm. "You and I have not had a great relationship, and it's mostly my fault. You are an artist. I'm a novelist. Can we have the same relationship that Cézanne and Zola have?"

"Those two have been friends for a long time—since their youth, I think. But no, Pierre, you and I won't have that relationship. They don't get along. Zola wrote a novel titled *The Masterpiece*, and people thought one character fit Cézanne, who says it didn't fit him. The artist in the novel behaved like a bad person. Are you going to misrepresent me? Or can you just tolerate me, like Cézanne does Zola?"

"Jean, I don't know what you are talking about. I'm a novelist, and you are an artist. I want us to be friends when we both get famous in our own fields of creating."

"Now, that's a wonderful goal. Which means I need to get to my studio. It has been nice talking with you."

Pierre stood silently, looking the other way. "Jean, it has been nice for me too. But there is a young lady waiting for me." Pierre waved and walked away.

Jean shouted, "Wait, Pierre! What about your novel? Do I get a copy?"

Pierre kept walking even faster. Jean felt disappointed, thinking he would not get an answer that day.

Sorry for the Bad News

Jean walked toward his studio and then decided to try to find Degas. He saw Émile Zola sitting in a café with a cup of tea. Zola waved to Jean and invited him to join him.

Jean gladly sat at the table. After they exchanged greetings, Jean asked, "Where is Pierre now, Émile? I saw him earlier but forgot to ask him if I would get a copy of his novel. He walked off, saying he had to meet a lady. I'm only asking because some time ago, he said he would be giving me a copy of his novel. I like to read novels, and I like yours."

"You won't be getting a copy of Pierre's novel. They've all been burned, except for a few copies used in court."

Jean put his hands to his forehead and looked up at the sky. "Court? Now what?"

"Plagiarism. More than two-thirds of his novel is a direct copy of a novel published in Spain ten years ago. I know that because he stole my copy and then put it back. His publisher had him arrested. The Spanish author's editor registered the book in France. I'll probably know more next time I see you. I have to leave now. Sorry for the bad news about Pierre. By the way, are you a strong Catholic? Or another religion?"

"No. I grew up Catholic, like most French children. Why do you ask?"

"I thought you looked upset when you left the café when I talked about Lourdes and miracles. I'm good at reading people. Were you?"

"Yes. I heard you did see a miracle. Are you going to work that into your novel? I hope not. Anyway, it didn't affect my faith, which is dormant and doesn't depend on miracles. I'm fine. I haven't even thought about it since that night."

"Lots of people need to believe in miracles, not only at Lourdes. As for what I saw at Lourdes, no, it won't be in the novel. I'm a novelist and write what I want."

"I see you are a novelist, and novels are fiction, so I don't have to trust you."

"*Trust*, Jean, is a word that has some unpleasantness when used negatively."

"Words are your business, Mr. Zola. I'm an artist. People don't have to trust that my art exactly reproduces what I saw. The test is whether or not people like it."

"I have seen enough of your art to know I like it."

"So I will read your novel. I hope I like it."

"I need to be going. We can talk more later." Zola paid his bill and left.

Jean declined a drink when a waitress approached him. He resumed his effort to find Degas.

I'm Looking for a Subject

Jean didn't find Degas, so he went to the Café de la Nouvelle Athénes a bit early and helped several other artists pull the tables together and put chairs in place. When Degas came in, he quickly agreed to have Jean take lessons from him. "You will learn there is more to art than light and color."

Jean declined to continue that conversation. He did note that

Degas protected the two chairs on his right side between himself and Jean.

A few minutes later, Emille and Luisa came in. After looking at the group, Emille sat next to Jean, and Luisa took the other empty chair next to Degas. He stood up to greet each lady, but none of the other artists stood up, as they should have when a lady joined a table. Then, to Jean's surprise, Monet came into the café, and all of them except Degas stood up. Monet wore the same white suit and tan hat he'd had on when Jean last saw him painting in Giverny. He walked around the tables, greeting each of them. Neither lady extended her hand, so he didn't offer to shake hands. He did tip his hat to them both.

Monet took a seat and nodded to Cézanne. "What is the topic, Paul? Are we debating something important?"

"No, Claude, we're just having light conversation. You would have heard us when you came in if the subject related to something important."

"Well, I'm here because when I'm in Paris, I like to visit with my artist friends. Jean, I'll be here in Paris tomorrow on business, but there is garden work for you at the gardens. Can you make it the day after tomorrow?"

"Certainly," he replied, watching the expression on everyone's face. Some wondered how Jean could have so strong of a relationship with Monet.

Degas said he had been hoping Jean would take some lessons from him. "Others are," he said, pointing to the ladies.

Monet reminded them that Jean worked as a gardener for him and would do some of that work as well as learning more about painting. "Outside."

Turning to Emille, Jean asked, "And how are you getting along with Edgar?"

Cézanne spoke before she could respond. "If last evening is any indication, I hope they are doing better than they did then."

"We didn't know about absinthe," Luisa said quickly. "We don't have it in Philadelphia."

"We're drinking wine today," Emille added. "Red wine. Mr. Degas helped us get home last night. And we had another lesson with him today."

"And tomorrow," Degas said. He told them the address of the studio where they were to meet him tomorrow.

Jean watched Emille and Luisa pour more wine from the bottle they were sharing. Degas looked at him and said, "How is your painting life, Jean? What are you working on?"

"This afternoon, I sold that painting of the tree I did in Giverny." Jean nodded to Monet as well as to Degas. "I'm looking for a subject. I've done portraits." He pointed to his paintings on the wall. "Right now, I'm struggling with whether I paint inside or outside. I like both."

"Your self-portrait is nice," Emille said, patting his shoulder.

"So is your portrait of the woman," Luisa said. Each had affirmed the painting he'd seen her standing in front of earlier that week.

Monet and Degas both spoke at the same time.

"Outside," Monet said loudly.

"Inside!" Degas shouted.

Cézanne said, "It depends on what and where the topic of the painting takes you."

"Thank you both, gentlemen. Now you can see my struggle. But since I will be gardening for a while, I'll be outside. Probably."

Everyone laughed, and they went on to another topic. Jean had hoped Degas and Monet would debate the choice for him, but other artists had their topics in mind. Emille and Luisa only stayed long enough to finish their wine. He left a while after they did.

We Just Experienced Something Distasteful

Luisa and Emille had to ask several people in Montmartre where they could find the studio where Degas had said they would have their next lesson. Finally, they went to the rue Saint-Vincent on the level of the cabaret Lapin Agile. The street had more people painting than they had seen ever before. A man sitting on a chair with an easel in front of him told them which side of the road the studio was on. They both liked his painting of an old stone building behind several trees. Emille thought he captured the nature of Montmartre.

They found the studio in a few minutes. Emille knocked on the door, and they heard Degas tell them to come in. When the two ladies came inside and saw Degas, they both screamed in horror. Emille turned and covered her eyes. Luisa stared in disbelief. Degas was painting a nude model, who sat on a couch. She didn't move when the ladies screamed.

"Relax, Luisa. Calm down, Emille. This is a model. What is your name again, dear? I got so wrapped up in my painting I forgot your name."

"Call me any name you want. And who are these women?" The model leaned forward, disrupting her pose, not trying to cover herself.

"These ladies are new students of mine and have come for a lesson. I have been debating in my mind if I should have you stay so I can instruct them on why the human body needs to be understood by aspiring artists. Or perhaps each of them will take a turn at modeling—nude, of course."

Emille ran back outside. Luisa told him that neither of them had ever seen a naked woman, and there was no way they ever could accept it, even if it was important to some artists. "That's not who we are. And I would never pose nude for you or anyone. You are not going to be our instructor."

Luisa left and joined Emille outside. They hurried down the road, almost running, no longer looking at what the street artists were painting.

"Where are we going, Luisa?"

"To the Café de la Nouvelle Athénes. I need a glass of wine. And no absinthe."

When they reached the café, they rushed to a table. The waitress, Camille, came over to them and took their order. "You ladies look upset. Is something wrong?"

"Nothing is wrong. We just experienced something distasteful." Luisa smiled at Camille and patted Emille's arm. Then Luisa let out a gasp. "Where are Jean's paintings? The ones that hung up there?" She pointed to the empty spaces.

"I just took them down. Mr. Jean will be coming for them in a short while. He said something about selling them. I'll get your wine now."

Luisa and Emille looked at each other. Emille said, "You know, Luisa, artists buy other artists' paintings. It's what we have done with the Monet painting."

When Camille brought the wine, she affirmed that the paintings were for sale. She named the price for each. After she poured each of them a glass of wine, she offered to bring the paintings to them.

Luisa took the painting of the woman, and Emille took Jean's self-portrait. Neither had any comment on the other's choice. They sipped their wine, studying the paintings. Emille said Jean used good technique, as if he had been a student of Degas. "I remember now. Jean has had lessons from Degas."

Luisa agreed, pointing to the sleeves on the lady in the painting she held. Then Jean came into the café.

"Hello, ladies. You have my paintings. Do you want to buy them?" He walked over to their table, pointed to a chair, and sat down when they nodded that he would be welcome to join them.

"I have seen that artists buy the work of other artists. Remember the paintings by Cézanne and others that Monet has? He has a Degas, I believe." Emille looked to Luisa for affirmation.

"Yes, they do that," Jean said, hoping one or both of the ladies would want his paintings. "I have one Degas and two by Monet. And a few others."

"Yes, we want them. And perhaps you can guide us to find another art instructor?"

"What happened to Degas?"

"Don't ask," Emille said.

"All right, ladies. Why don't you again visit Mr. Monet? I know a place where you can stay a lot cheaper than the hotel where you were. I'm going to Giverny in the morning. By train."

Both ladies had taken money from their purses. Luisa said, "Here you are, Mr. Jean. We'll join you on the train in the morning."

Like an Echo of Her Body

Jean felt good about the promise that the ladies would join him on the train to Giverny in the morning. What did that leave him for the rest of the day? It felt too early for more wine. He gave Camille a tip and went to find Degas. He knew where Degas likely would be since he'd overheard Degas tell the ladies at the café last night where they would meet him that day, and he knew the studio.

He walked quickly, pausing only to look at the canvas of a man painting an old stone building behind several trees. "Your perspective is very well done," Jean said, and the artist smiled. Jean then walked up to the studio where Degas had said he would be. He reached for the door to knock on it, when he heard a woman scream and Degas, whose voice he recognized, shouting. He could hear scuffling, so he went inside. Degas lay on top of a nude woman he recognized as a model who posed nude. "Sorry. I'll wait outside," he said.

"I'll be done soon," Degas replied.

Outside the studio, Jean walked in circles in front of the door. After a short while, the model came out, mostly dressed and angry. "Did he pay you?" he asked.

Her look of contempt surprised him. "He paid me to model. What do you think I am?" She hurried away, not caring what his answer would be, not expecting he could imagine an answer of any decency. He watched her stomp down the street, swinging her arms and clenching her fists. Did he feel sad for her? He couldn't say that. She had a reputation, and she knew Degas did also.

He gave Degas a bit of time to get himself together and then went inside. Degas sat on a chair, brushing his hair. He pointed to another chair, so Jean sat there.

"What do you want, Jean?"

"Edgar, I thought I'd talk to you about my painting inside. You were quite positive when you shouted at Monet after he said I should paint outside. Your thinking is important to me."

"And tomorrow or sometime soon you're going to Giverny to work for him, and you'll have him teach you more about painting en plein air. I'm not a fool."

"That's right; you aren't a fool. I came here to get your opinion because I respect it. I own one of your paintings. I admire your art as being at the top of what is being produced in this time." He stood and walked to Degas's partially completed painting of the nude. "You have used circles nicely to define her. She is so real."

Degas got out of his chair and came over to the painting. "You mean these circles," he said, running his finger over parts of the woman. "I liked your portrait of that woman and the self-portrait. The ones at the café. Clearly, they are proof you are capable of painting inside. With some proper lessons, you could get much better." He picked up a brush and his palette, looked at the painting, and moved his brush over parts of the painting without touching it. Then he put some paint on the brush and put circles in the cloth the model sat on, almost like an echo of her body. He frowned. "I don't know if I'll be able to finish this. She should know the painting brings out emotion in me. And she couldn't claim to be a virgin."

"I didn't think she would be." Jean mentally looked for what else needed to be done. "I don't see why you'd need her again. Now that you have firsthand memories of her totally."

"I do. And the last time we had one of these sessions, it took her over a month to come back. Just to model, so she said. I don't want to wait that long."

They talked for a while more, discussing inside art. Jean mentioned the painter at the start of the street. Degas said he knew the artist. "He's done that scene at least a dozen times. Won't let me correct what he's doing wrong."

Jean replied that the painting seemed to be fine, particularly the perspective. Degas did not reply. Jean left the studio without saying anything.

You Should Not Drink Alone

After Jean left the café, Luisa and Emille sat holding the paintings they'd bought from him. Camille stopped at their table and looked at each painting for a moment. "You ladies both seem quite convinced you have the better one. No, not better but the one that appeals to you the most. Which is fine. In fact, it's very nice that each of you has the painting you like best. We all have likes. And dislikes." She pointed to his self-portrait. "Jean is an attractive man—that's for sure. But he likes the ladies a lot. In fact, that's all I know about him. We've never gone out together."

Luisa laughed. "Camille, would you go out with him? Would your boss let you go out with any of the regular customers?"

Camille stepped back from their table and went to the bar.

Emille held up the portrait and moved it back and forth as if to see Jean's sides. "What I like best is how he used his clothing— some very fine clothing—to bring the focus to his personality. Look at the crease in his trousers. It's like the painting is saying, 'Here I am,' or something. It invites the viewer to want to talk with him."

"Talk?" Luisa said, laughing even louder. "He's asking you, the viewer, to do more than talk. That's what Camille was saying. He likes the ladies a lot. Well, this lady does not like him back. I would not have bought that portrait. And don't think that I bought this one of the woman because I wanted to please him. I haven't fallen for him like you did."

Camille came back from the bar and listened to their conversation. Before Emille could reply to Luisa, Camille asked, "Why do you like that portrait of the lady? A very nicely endowed lady, I might add. And would either of you like another glass of wine? My shift ends soon."

Camille didn't wait for an answer; she went off to the bar. Emille said she didn't think she wanted another glass. Luisa thought for a moment and then said she would drink the wine. "You can give yours to Camille," she said, laughing.

"What's so funny?" Camille said, putting a glass of wine by each lady.

Emille stood up. "Luisa, you should not drink alone. Camille, you can have my glass of wine. You can talk about her painting by Jean. I'll see you back at the apartment, Luisa." She turned and walked out without looking back.

Camille went back to the bar and talked for a bit to the bartender. Her replacement was due soon, and there weren't any other customers. She came back to Luisa and sat where Emille had been sitting. "I'm done with my shift. I don't drink while working, so this will be a very nice treat. May I hold your painting?"

Luisa handed it to her and then picked up her glass to toast Camille.

They touched their glasses lightly, and each took a sip of the wine. "The clothing the woman is wearing is quite nice, as though she is well to do. Mr. Jean did a nice job of focusing on this part," Camille said, touching the bodice. "I suppose if it had been a painting of a nude, he would have had more difficulty focusing our attention like that. But maybe we might look at her anyway. Have you ever seen a nude woman?"

Luisa nodded and then closed her eyes and covered them with her hands. "Today. The only time in my life. At Degas's studio. He was painting a nude model, and I was shocked. Emille immediately covered her eyes and then ran out. I just looked at the woman. Don't tell anyone I said this, but I looked at her breasts. Degas tried to tell me it is necessary to understand the human body to paint nudes. Does Jean do that?" Luisa gulped the rest of her wine.

"I don't know much about Mr. Jean other than the two paintings, and he is good at playing cards. He doesn't get loud when the artists argue. I think this painting you bought shows what he thinks about women but remains modest. Here is your painting. Go. Go to your apartment. You need to relax."

"I will, but neither of us should rush the wine. Let's just say this is the last glass."

At Least She Had a Smile

Emille walked toward her apartment, not in any hurry and not paying attention to what she passed by, holding the painting by her side. Suddenly, she heard her name.

"Emille! Emille, how are you doing?"

She looked up and saw Jean, who was not as formally dressed as in the painting of him she carried. She stopped, looked at him, and frowned. Then she started to cry.

Jean walked up to her. He wanted to comfort her, hold her, and pat her shoulders, but he stayed back from touching her. He offered her a handkerchief, which she took. She wiped her face and then stared at him.

"Emille, why are you crying? What happened?"

"I don't know how to say this. Well, I do know how; I just don't know if I can."

He walked closer to her and offered her his right arm to comfort her without excessive contact. She held on to his arm and leaned against him, still sobbing.

"Emille, don't cry. Or cry—I'm fine with that. I'm here to help you. What's wrong?" He waited as her sobbing eased.

She turned more toward him. Then she stepped back. "Remember back at the café when we told you not to ask why we were upset? Luisa and I went to the studio to have a lesson with Degas. He had been painting a nude woman. She didn't even try to cover herself when we saw her. I ran out of the studio. Luisa stayed for a short time, and then we hurried to the café to recover. I have never seen a naked woman. A nude. I'm so shocked. I hate men."

Jean tried to smile but couldn't. "You hate men? Have I ever asked you to model in the nude? Of course not. I haven't even asked you if I could paint your portrait, though I would like that honor. I'll ask that some other day. Has Mr. Monet ever asked you to paint a nude? Not even a dressed model. The answer is no."

Emille continued to dry her tears with his handkerchief. "You are right. The answer is no."

"Emille, I don't want to compare Degas with Mr. Monet, but Monet's paintings don't need naked women like Degas paints. Degas is into indoor painting. I just talked to him at his studio, and by the way, he finally answered my question about painting inside. He has painted—and sold for nice sums of francs—quite a few nude women. It is art. When I look at them, I see art. But don't worry; I also understand what you see. Degas also paints ballet dancers. In fact, some of his nude models are ballet dancers. But my point is that Mr. Monet doesn't paint nudes. I don't think he ever painted a nude lady. You do know that his painting titled *Impression Sunrise* is where impressionism came from, right?"

"What's your point, Jean?" Emille now had her arms crossed, standing tall with her chin pointed at him. "Men paint naked women. Okay, Mr. Monet hasn't done so or hasn't released one. Why not? Have you?"

He shook his head and looked into her eyes for a moment. "The answer to both of those questions is the same. Mr. Monet sees the world as an artist. He definitely likes women, and I have to admit he hasn't been faithful to Alice, whom he had an affair with during his marriage to Camille. And I like women. I painted the self-portrait you have in your hands so women would be attracted to me at my best. And something might happen. But my personal life and my being an artist are kept separate. Both Mr. Monet and I are artists. Our personal lives don't end up on canvas. Emille, let me walk you home, and then I'll go my own way. Okay?" He gestured for her to walk on the inside as he moved to the curb.

Before she moved, Emille held up his self-portrait. "Someday I want to wear that scarf you have on. I like the purple, and the silk looks soft. And are you walking me to my apartment as an artist? Or is this personal life?"

He sighed, noting at least she had a smile. "I don't have a canvas or a palette. I'm just walking you home. Nothing else." He thought about what he'd just said. "Nothing else, as I said, but whatever you have in mind."

When they reached her apartment, she patted his shoulder and went inside. Jean went home. Neither of them mentioned tomorrow's train ride.

What These Ladies Are Painting

That evening, Jean went back to the Café de la Nouvelle Athénes and got there early enough again to help move the tables and arrange the chairs for the evening's exchange of art thoughts at the café. He and those he helped put the tables near the wall, leaving room for the chairs where some artists would have their backs to the wall. They joked about that idea. Slowly at first and then in a hurry, the artists arrived and took their places. Their conversation had little substance, as they focused more on ordering their drinks than being profound about art.

That evening, a respected Parisian artist named William-Adolphe Bouguereau joined the others at the table. Bouguereau didn't regularly come to the café because he often had students at that hour of the evening. He taught painting and drawing at the Académie Julian to both men and women. One of his favorite students, Gabrielle de Veaux Clements, had exhibited at the Paris Salon in 1885. She had kept in touch with Bouguereau over the years, mostly as gratitude for his teaching. Jean thought about recommending him to Luisa and Emille.

After Bouguereau settled into his chair and ordered his absinthe, he waved a piece of paper at the group. "I have another letter from Gabrielle Clements. She and her friend Ellen Hale have bought a house together. It's been years that those two have been together. Both are good artists too."

Degas laughed. "They are totally open about their Boston marriage, aren't they? Well, you would know." He looked at the other artists. "How many of you get letters from your students that many years after they went somewhere else? How many of you have women students who live in a Boston marriage? If so, how do they spend time together?"

Jean laughed and said it had become the other way around for him. "Monet sends me letters whenever he has gardening for me to do. And as far as spending time together, the couple I know, two lovely ladies, seem to be totally focused on painting."

Bouguereau looked at the other artists. "Yes, I would know, Edgar. I knew back when I taught Clements, when Hale came to Paris to be with her. Who cares about them as a couple or if it is a Boston marriage? I don't."

Pissarro slammed his hand on the table. "Who cares about the sex lives of two women? Change the subject, or I'm going home. After another absinthe." He waved to the waiter who had been serving the group. Then he relaxed, smiling at the regulars. "You all know me. I'm peaceful. I just did the hand thing for fun. What I really wanted to say is that we should be interested in what these ladies are painting, not doing."

"I can tell you that, sir." Bouguereau also signaled to the waiter for another absinthe. "Miss Clements has also written in this letter that she has been commissioned to paint a mural for the 1893 World's Columbian Exposition in Chicago, though she didn't say where it would be placed. She also is painting a mural for the New Century Club in Philadelphia. Hale fell ill and spent a year in Santa Barbara, California. She's back with Clements and will show some of her work at the same Chicago Columbian Exposition. All that plus the home they share."

"That is impressive. Murals take a lot of thought. And energy." Degas lifted his arm up high, exaggerating the effort of reaching the top of a mural. "Does she paint like you do? Traditional? Modern mocking of classical stuff, like women's bodies?"

Pissarro finished his new drink and stood up. "I did say I would leave, and I am leaving to go to bed. Not because of this conversation. I have a very early landscape to start tomorrow. Before dawn. Thanks for your friendships." He went to the bar to pay his bill and then waved as he left the café.

Bouguereau sipped his drink. "I'm glad Pissarro came here tonight."

Jean thought about touching him on the shoulder to affirm what he had shared with the group.

Degas moved to sit in a chair more distant from Bouguereau. He knew that if he didn't say anything and let the other artists think about Bouguereau's style of painting, they all might get up to leave. "Mr. Bouguereau, you are not an impressionist, and yet we let you join us."

Bouguereau stood. "The novelist Émile Zola is not even a painter, and you let him join you. And what about those two women you've been teaching at the Louvre? Good night, gentlemen."

Jean didn't follow Bouguereau when he went to the bar to pay his bill. He looked at Degas and tried to understand why Degas insulted Bouguereau's style of painting. Then he shrugged, seeing it as trying to keep the public focused on impressionism. Nobody had much to say, and one by one, they all left. He hoped next time would be different and then wondered how Luisa and Emille would have reacted to that evening.

You Don't Mind Riding Backward

Jean arrived at the Saint-Lazare station a few minutes before the scheduled departure time. The engine had already started building up steam. He saw the difference between smoke and steam and then hurried on board, bringing his bag, three canvases, and his paints and palette. He had left his easel at home.

When he got on board, he felt happy to see Emille and Luisa sitting across the aisle from each other with their luggage next to them on the seats. He had hoped they had come to the station earlier. He stood there for a moment, trying to decide where he should sit. Luisa pointed to the seat in front of her, suggesting he move the back so he could face her. Emille made no similar motion, so he sat facing Luisa.

"I know you don't mind riding backward," Luisa said, smiling.

Emille also smiled at him when he sat down. He quickly concluded that the two ladies had talked about his bringing Emille home last night. He returned their smiles and leaned back to relax.

After a few minutes, Luisa asked Jean, "Would you ever consider coming to Philadelphia? It is quite different from Paris but very interesting. Our history is on display, and the art museum is very nice."

"I'd like to cross the ocean on a ship. And France had the pleasure of being the USA's first ally."

Neither of the ladies said more. Jean wondered if either one would let him visit. Would he ever want to meet the parents of one of those lovely ladies?

The sun didn't shine that day, so looking out the window didn't have the appeal of multiple colors. In any case, as an artist, he preferred looking at the ladies. He glanced at Luisa and then at Emille. They looked at each other and then down at their feet. Luisa wore a solid blue dress with sleeves just to her forearms. Her blue hat had a flower on the front, by the brim. Her blue belt emphasized her slimness. Emille wore a gold skirt and a brown blouse with a brown jacket that had a strip of cloth that matched the skirt. Her brown hat included a blue flower. "You both look very nice. Are those dresses you found in Paris?" He wanted to say something to get a conversation going. Both ladies smiled without replying but also adjusted their skirts to make sure they covered their ankles. He knew he shouldn't bring up the nude model they'd seen at the studio where Degas painted. He especially wouldn't tell them what he'd seen.

He settled back, feeling the up-and-down movement of the train. After a while, he pretended to drift off to sleep. He had his eyes closed but ears open in case they talked. He began to feel drowsy and thought he might have a nap. He braced his elbows to keep himself sitting upright.

Emille spoke first after she thought Jean had fallen asleep. "Like I told you, Luisa, Jean does not come on strong at all. He's just, well, there—like he's waiting."

"What or whom is he waiting for? You? Me? No, not me."

"Why not you? He seems to like us both, in a respectful way. If he came from Philadelphia, I would say he is cultured. And even though he is French, he's like a lot of men I have met back home."

Luisa didn't say anything, but he presumed she either nodded or shook her head. Neither lady said more while he remained awake. The rhythm of the train easily put him to sleep.

When they arrived at the station in Vernon, Jean woke up, yawned, and stretched.

"We're almost there, Mr. Jean," Luisa said. "How did your rest go? Didn't you get enough sleep last night?"

Emille looked out her window.

"Oh, Miss Luisa, I just felt the rhythm of the train. A nap makes the time go faster. I hope I didn't prevent you ladies from talking to each other."

"We didn't have much to say. Emille and I are anxious to meet Mr. Monet again. At breakfast, we agreed to totally follow whatever he says."

They carried their bags and boxes to the shuttle without any difficulty. Again, he sat facing both ladies. They did not have a conversation with him on the shuttle other than to point to the hay bales they'd seen on their first ride to Giverny. Each of them knew that Monet would dominate whatever happened on their visit.

The Room Next Door

When they arrived at Giverny, they walked to the entrance of Monet's house and sat on the green benches. Once again, Jean sat facing the ladies. Monet's wife, Alice, came out and greeted them, and Jean felt pleased to get a gentle hug from her, especially with the two ladies watching. After some polite conversation, Alice asked him to take the ladies to the hotel. He said he had a less expensive place for them at a house owned by one of the residents. "It's also closer than the hotel." He stood up and bowed to Alice.

"I have no problem with that. My husband is talking with some of the gardeners now, so this would be a good time to put your things where you will be staying. You all will be welcome for dinner at about sunset. There will be no lesson today, though Claude hardly ever talks about anything but painting. And his garden. Jean, you might go find him after you have your things in your room. You ladies can stroll the gardens if you like." Alice curtsied and went back into the house.

No one spoke after Alice left. Jean led the ladies down a brick path beyond Monet's gardens. After about five minutes of walking, they came to a large brick structure with six windows on the second floor, which he knew were bedroom windows. The same number of rooms were on the back half of the apartment building.

The red tiles contrasted nicely with the bricks. The windows all had black shutters.

They walked from the brick path to a nicely compacted sand-filled yard surrounded by bushes, plants, and flowers. Emille went to some peonies and smelled them. The three of them stopped by a small metal table for two. Luisa tapped Emille's shoulder. "Emille, we can have tea together without any room for someone else." She smiled at Jean.

He chuckled and said, "I could have tea with one of you at a time." Neither lady smiled.

He suggested they walk up the six steps to the entrance. The owner, Madame Baudy, expected them because of his telegram. She had them fill out registration papers and waved at Jean, who had given her that information much earlier. She took the three of them up the stairs to the second floor and gave a key to each lady as they entered their room, which had two single beds, a desk with a chair, and a second chair. The window faced out to the back of the building, but neither lady bothered to see the view.

Then Madame Baudy led Jean to the room next door and gave him his key. He went to the window to see if he had the same view to the west that he had at his gardener friend's house. He did. He put his stuff away and left to find Monet.

Luisa opened her door and asked him to bring greetings to Mr. Monet. "We're going to walk in his gardens. We love those green benches."

He gave her a thumbs-up and went out to the brick road. He had an idea of where the gardeners were working and wanted to see his friend Leon.

Pretend It's a Painting

Jean found the gardeners at the point where the River Epte came closest to a large pond that had been dug out while he spent time in

Paris. He waved to all the gardeners and went to Leon. They shook hands. Then Jean acknowledged Monet with a wave.

"Jean, welcome back. Leon, Jean is back in charge. Fill him in on what we have done when you have time today."

Leon walked up to Monet. "Sir, that is fine. He paints too, so he can talk gardens with you." Leon turned to Jean. "We needed to have Mr. Monet make a decision about a tree, or we would have stopped working."

"What tree?" Jean tried not to laugh.

"It's gone. It blocked the way of a straight-line path for the pond."

"That's enough. I'll also show you the painting, Jean. First, go over to those trees with Leon, and have him explain how I want the connection to the river to let water into the pond. At least he didn't interrupt my art with a shovel in his hands. And you won't either. Gardening is gardening, and art is art." Monet took off his wide-brimmed hat and wiped the perspiration off his bald head. He squinted, looking up at the sun. "Time for me to do art. Do what you are to do as a gardener. You can do art later."

"Claude, the pond looks great. Someday folks are going to praise your gardens as much as they praise your art now." Jean waved to Leon, and they walked over to the trees Monet had pointed to. The pond had been dug, so some of the trees' roots were exposed. He asked Leon if Monet wanted to save them or not.

"All I know, Jean, is that Monet said they won't survive like they are. He's been waiting for you to get here. We're supposed to suggest what to do but not do it until he tells us to do whatever we suggest."

"Not doing it is the easy part. The hard part is deciding what to do. Leon, does the pond have places where it gets wider or narrower?"

"Yes. There's a place where he wants to put a bridge of some kind over the pond, and we made that nicely narrow. Some of the guys are making paths to the spot."

"Let's stand back where the river is. I'm going to imagine it is a painting."

When they walked to the river where it would pour water into the pond, Jean tried to focus on what it would look like on a canvas. The clump of trees would form a line from where he stood pointing to the part of the pond beyond where he could see. He used his hands and thumbs to locate where the frame would be. Then he stepped back and turned to Leon. "We keep the trees. I'll tell Monet that the clump of trees looks like it is saluting the pond itself. Now, you figure out how to get the dirt back in to cover the roots."

Leon slapped him on the back, saying, "It takes an artist to see what an artist wants to see." He went off to see what the other gardeners were doing.

Jean promised to tell him what Monet said when he said it. Jean made the frame with his hands again just to be sure the trees did what he said they did. Then he said, "It takes an artist to see what an artist wants to see."

Use Your Knowledge of Art to Solve a Gardening Question

Jean caught up with Monet as Monet finished packing up the painting he had been working on. Jean picked up the easel and followed Monet into the studio. He knew Monet had a private studio as well as that one and assumed he finally had finished that painting and intended to put it in storage. Instead, Monet told Jean to put up the easel when they were inside. Then Monet put the painting on the easel.

"Jean, you haven't seen this painting. It is another version of the cathedral in Rouen. You've seen some of the others. What's different about this one? If you remember them."

Jean took his time studying the painting, trying to remember what he had seen and paying Monet for the time he took to evaluate a work of art. He copied Monet's way of looking at the painting from different perspectives. "Claude, the sky isn't as blue as I remember. Clouds aren't blocking the sun here, but they are causing the sunlight to be diffused. There is the glow of the sun but no shadows."

"Very good, Jean." As Monet spoke, they heard a voice, presumably Alice's, calling to him to come in for dinner. "Very good. I hear that my wife is telling us that dinner is ready. Shall we respond? And by the way, there are a few other differences in this version of the cathedral that are only obvious if you have one of the others to compare it to. I'll get one out and show you later. Right now, I'm hungry."

On the walk to the dining room, Jean told Monet what he had decided for the trees by the river. He told him he had envisioned the scene as a painting and seen the line of trees saluting the pond.

"Jean, I did the same when I looked at it before you showed up. I wanted to see if you would use your knowledge of art to solve a gardening question. I'm quite pleased that you solved it the same way I did. Tell Leon and the others to fill in the roots." Monet reached the steps to the house before Jean did, so Jean showed a nice smile.

They walked up the steps and into the dining room, where Alice and the two ladies were sitting where they had last time they'd all dined there. Alice stood up to greet the men, but the two ladies remained seated. Jean wondered if they'd had a conversation with Alice or were just tired from walking in the gardens. What would they talk to Alice about? Not him, he decided.

Monet settled into his chair and nodded at everyone. "Do you ladies from Philadelphia say a blessing for the food before eating? We French are Catholic, and even when or if we don't bother to worship, we do follow some of the traditions. This is one of them. I know we didn't bless the lunch you had last time you visited, but this is dinner. Would either of you like to bless this dinner? And by the way, what is your religious tradition?"

"I'm Presbyterian," Emille replied.

"I'm Episcopalian, which is Anglican in the United Kingdom. I would be honored to bless the meal," Luisa said.

The server brought in a Roquefort and caramelized onion tart. When Monet nodded to her, Luisa began the prayer. "Holy Father, bless this meal and our lives to your service."

They all were silent except for Emille, who said, "Amen."

The tart tasted nice, as did the oyster soup that came next, with its small oysters. The main course of salmon with a creamy, earthy truffle sauce tasted spectacularly delicious. Jean thought he had eaten all he could, savoring each of the courses. Then the server brought in chocolate and pistachio ice cream, his favorite flavor combination. Several times, he rubbed his stomach while pulling it in to assure himself that the meal had not spoiled his figure. Some time ago, he had learned that women looked at that.

The five of them had little conversation during the meal. That surprised Jean because Monet always talked about art, particularly at dinner. He noticed that the server came in with the next course before they had finished the one they were eating. It occurred to Jean that Alice wanted the meal to be over as soon as possible. As soon as everyone had finished eating the ice cream, she got out of her chair, thanked the artists for joining them, and excused herself. The two ladies thanked Monet for the meal, as did Jean.

Jean walked the ladies back to the apartment house where they were staying. They didn't say much then either. He didn't ask about their garden walk, but he did ask if they believed in miracles. "What do your denominations say about miracles?"

"Why do you want to know? Emille asked.

"I had a conversation with the novelist Émile Zola. He's writing a novel about Lourdes and is leaving out a miracle he actually saw happen."

Emille laughed at Jean. "He's a writer of fiction and can write what he wants. Does he have any of his books translated into English?"

Jean didn't reply. When they got to the entrance, no one said anything about the table for two or anything else. The ladies went inside, while Jean thought about visiting Leon for some wine and friendship.

Did You See Me in That Mirror?

Luisa and Emille went up the stairs to their room. Jean tipped his hat to them and told them he planned to go see a friend. In truth, he hoped Leon had some wine. He and Leon liked to sit outside when the weather felt nice and share a bottle.

When he arrived at Leon's house, it didn't surprise him that Leon sat at a table on the front porch. Jean saw a bottle of cabernet sauvignon wine, three glasses, and a relatively young woman he did not know.

Jean sat at the table, nodding to the woman.

"Jean, this lovely lady is a neighbor to me. Her name is Felise." Leon added that they were friends as well as neighbors, and then he poured wine into the glasses. They raised them in a toast to their friendship.

"Leon, thanks for the wine. It is nice," Jean said. "It is also my pleasure to meet you, Miss Felise. Oh, and, Leon, Monet approved keeping the trees. Tomorrow we'll get that done."

"Mr. Jean, do you work for Mr. Monet? He is my neighbor, but I don't know him. Leon says he is difficult to work for."

"Yes, I work for Mr. Monet. As a gardener like Leon. But my primary goal in life is to be an artist, and Mr. Monet is both a great artist and a great gardener. He is great at teaching both. He's got his way of doing things, and you do things that way, or he is difficult. He's a good man, but his focus that makes him great at art and gardens is so intense he has trouble with diversions. For example, he won't let his art students ask questions."

"Why not?" Felise asked.

Leon said, "That's why Jean told me about the trees we're going to keep in the pond, Felise. I wouldn't be able to ask Mr. Monet about what to do. Oh, Jean, how did you like dinner with him? I never got invited when I supervised the gardeners."

"It's because I'm an artist. The ladies were there too. He asked them both what religion they had. Both are Protestant, though different forms. The food was great, as always. Marguerite is a very fine chef, just like you are a very fine gardener. Claude does want the best."

They drank the wine quickly, recovering from Monet. Jean declined to share another bottle with Leon. He thanked his friend and then left Leon with Felise on the deck. They both looked pleased. They waited until Jean could no longer see them and then went inside, not for another bottle of wine.

When Jean got back to the apartment building, the ladies were sitting at the outside table for two. They had a bottle of cabernet sauvignon as well and, to his pleasure, had a third glass on the table. "Pour some wine for yourself," Emille said. "Luisa had the nice idea to bring it with us from Paris. But you might have to stand while you drink it."

Jean quickly poured himself a glass of the wine. "The two chairs are for romantic couples." He saw no reaction; both ladies just looked at him. "The apartment has a few more chairs behind this set of bushes. If you don't mind, I will join you."

He got a chair, sat down, and proposed a toast. "To art, always and forever." They touched glasses and sipped their wine.

Emille looked at Jean and leaned forward a bit. "To art. I like that. You do love art, I know. Does it interfere with other parts of your life? Does art limit what else you might do?" She leaned back and smiled. "It totally dominates what Mr. Monet does."

He looked around and then gazed at her. "Art alone does not totally dominate what he does. He's equally dominated by gardening. As for me, well, I did some work for the pond and talked with Mr. Monet. About gardening and art. I had time to go visit

Leon. I have time to sit with you two ladies. Lovely ladies, I might add. And thank you for the wine. It has good flavor." He didn't mention that Leon had served the same wine.

Luisa finished her glass of wine, stood up, and announced that she wanted to go in. "When you come in, Mr. Jean, you should put your chair back behind the bushes. This house apparently encourages romantic couples."

Emille sat for a while, sipping the last of the wine in her glass. Jean waited for her to say something, mostly because he couldn't think of anything he could or should say. Then she stood up also, saying, "I'm going in now too. When you finish the bottle, bring it inside. Good night."

He did as they'd asked him to do, putting the chair back, finishing the wine, and putting the bottle in the kitchen. He went upstairs to his room and heard the noise of a conversation but not what the ladies were in fact saying as he walked past their room.

Emille paced the room. "The bathroom is down the hall, and I planned to use that to change into my nightgown, but then I'd have to walk back exposed. I didn't bring a robe. Did you?"

"No, but don't worry. I'll go to the bathroom before changing and then change when you go to the bathroom. I'll step outside if you want. Really. If you don't trust me not to look as you change into your nightgown."

"I don't need to go to the bathroom. I did just before we went outside. I just want to change. Just look the other way."

Luisa had her back to Emille and could see her changing by looking at a mirror on the wall. Emille took off her dress and then her underwear.

Emille finished changing and turned to look at Luisa. "Oh Lord, did you see me in that mirror? I'm mortified."

"What mirror?" Luisa turned to look at Emille and then looked back at the wall where the mirror hung. "Oh, no. I focused on looking at the chairs, wishing I had sat down. Honest."

I Don't Need Your Comments

The next morning, Jean walked with the ladies to Monet's house. Monet had his easel and a canvas ready to paint. He motioned for the two ladies to sit on a green bench near where he had put his easel. Jean said hello and then excused himself to go supervise the gardeners' work on covering the tree roots.

"Ladies, make sure you can see my canvas. Your first lesson is to watch me paint."

Luisa and Emille sat on opposite ends of the bench so they could see the canvas and not just Monet's back. Monet looked at a wisteria tree and then began putting paint on the canvas. Both ladies were amazed at how quickly he went back and forth between looking at the tree and then adding two or three brushstrokes on the canvas. Monet worked quicker than any artist either lady had ever seen.

Luisa interrupted Monet after just a few minutes of watching. "Degas had us copy a Rembrandt, and he said I started with concern for the light coming in through the window. Emille started at the center, where the holy family sat."

"I'm not Degas, but I do know the painting. Indoors, of course. I am Claude Monet, and right now, you are my students, not his. Just watch. I don't need your comments."

The tree seemed to come to life as Monet, quickly looking at the tree then adding three or four more strokes with his brush, continued his work.

"Okay, ladies, now it is time to see if you were watching closely enough. I showed you how I paint. I know my subject and keep looking at it—in fact, in this case, only at the part of the tree I am going to paint next. Then I come back to the canvas, putting down what I have seen. Four brushstrokes are enough to show what I saw. If you, like so many artists, don't keep looking at the subject, you are using your imagination of what it looks like, not your vision. Did you see Degas paint? He sometimes has his students watch him, as I do. As most art teachers do. It is easier to show how to paint rather than to put it in words. Did you?"

"Yes, we saw him paint," Emille answered. "I think he positioned himself to see the Rembrandt just by looking up. He did not use his brush nearly as fast as you do. He used a finer brush, not a thick one like you use. His strokes were longer and slower."

Luisa agreed. "More graceful, as if he wanted to enter into a relationship with the painting." She hesitated and then added, "You seem to dominate the wisteria."

"That is totally not true. I do not dominate what I paint. I embrace it. I am taking the essence of my subject—in this case, the wisteria tree—and putting it on canvas so that anyone who sees the painting will also see that essence. Degas is a good artist. I don't want to get into a debate about his techniques. If you like him better, go back to him."

"I'm sorry, Mr. Monet. So is Emille. We came here to learn to paint from you. It's just that in our art schools back home in Pennsylvania, we are encouraged to ask questions and also make comments. It is how we learn. But we will watch you paint and listen to you as you teach us."

Both ladies wondered if anything in France was the same as back home. Then Emille whispered to Luisa, "There are eccentrics in both places, so don't worry."

Monet finished the wisteria tree painting in about an hour, or so the ladies thought. "I like this and will work on it again tomorrow morning when the light is right. I hope you learned something." He took the canvas and went to the studio. The ladies didn't know what they should do.

Luisa walked over to a nearby tree and bent to pick up a leaf. Monet came out of the studio, came back to them, and said, "Don't you know what you should do now?"

"I have some idea." Luisa held out the leaf to him. "Mr. Monet, this is a leaf from one of the maple trees here. Please paint the leaf. Here is my sketchbook."

Monet took the leaf and held it up to the sun. "This is how it looks on the tree." He took the sketchbook and put some green paint on the page. Then he added a stroke of red and two strokes of yellow to define the stem and the three extensions into the leaf. More strokes diluted some of the green. Other colors were used to darken more of the green. The ladies were amazed. Monet then extended the green to form the edges of the leaf. He held up the sketchbook for the ladies to see.

"That is amazing," Emille said. "It is so real."

"That's what she asked me to do. Paint the leaf, not something that isn't the leaf." Monet stepped back and then tore the page out of the sketchbook. "The painting and the leaf are mine. Here's your sketchbook."

Luisa took the sketchbook, handed it to Emille, and then moved toward Monet. "I want the leaf and the painting."

At that moment, Jean walked up. "Claude, what have you got there? Is that a sketchbook page?" Jean looked at the page when Monet held it up. "Did you teach them how to do that?"

"Yes, he taught us how to paint the leaf. But now he won't give it to me. I need the painting and the leaf to remember what he taught us." Luisa stepped back, no longer threatening to force Monet to give her the page.

"I am an artist," Monet said, moving closer to his easel. "I get paid for my work."

Emille spoke up. "Mr. Monet, you are our instructor. You are teaching us to be artists. You've been paid to do that. Please reconsider giving Luisa her page. She, and I, will use it to remember what you showed us. Then she'll give it back to you if you still want it."

"Claude, she does have a good point," Jean said, pointing to Emille. "You didn't sign it, did you? If not, it won't be worth much if they try to sell it. Who would want it anyway, other than these two students of yours?"

"Jean, go back to your gardening work. I'll give in to your argument," Monet said, handing the paper to Luisa and crumpling the leaf.

Jean did leave, not wanting to be crumpled by Monet.

As If to See into the Future?

Under Leon's direction, the gardeners had dragged a large wagon full of soil to put in the pond to cover the roots of the trees before the water was let into the pond. Jean got there before they started to shovel the dirt. "Hold it, friends. If we just put soil over the roots, it will wash away when we let the water in. Find two or three bushes, and plant them in the pond next to the roots before the water reaches the soil. Put two or three more bushes at the other end as well, to anchor the soil."

Leon clapped his hands in affirmation of the advice. He didn't tell anyone he'd had the same plan in mind.

Jean saw two of the gardeners get into the pond and take bushes from the others who were digging them up. They dug deep holes so the roots would be safe. They compressed the soil around the bush roots. They looked up at Jean when they were done. "Well done," he told them. "Leon, let's get the tree roots covered in soil now."

The gardeners formed a line from the wagon to the tree roots, handing buckets full of dirt and putting the dirt over the tree roots as well as the bush roots. Leon and Jean took the empty buckets back to the wagon. It took more than an hour to empty the wagon. Leon and Jean agreed they didn't need any more soil. Plus, they were exhausted.

"Okay, friends, time for lunch and a bit of relaxation. I'm going to see what Mr. Monet wants next. I'm guessing he'll want to have a celebratory event when we let the water in. Leon, let's walk the whole length of the pond to see if any more needs to be done."

It took them about half an hour to walk the pond to where it ended near Monet's house. Jean said, "Leon, you and your crew did a great job. I can just imagine the pond full of water and loaded with water lilies."

"Thank you, Jean. Mr. Monet supervised quite a bit of the time. He kept stepping back and moving his hands as if to see into the future when the lilies are planted. He also kept looking at the sun. Several of us saw him come back to the pond after we were done for the day. He still looked at the sun."

"No surprise there. And who is waiting for us where the pond ends? Hello, Claude!" Jean shouted, and they both waved. Monet waved back and then turned to his canvas as he waited for them to get to him.

As they approached Monet's easel, he put down his brush. "I see, Jean, that once again, you are doing what I would have done. Putting rocks to protect the tree roots is good. Does the pond look like it should?"

"No, sir."

"What? What is wrong? Tell me."

"Claude, I'm just joking. The pond is fine, but it needs water and plants to look like it should."

Monet looked at him for a moment and then laughed. "I don't always get your humor, Jean, when I have so much invested in the project. Emotional investment. But you are right. It needs water and plants. See how, when I stand here, I will be facing the sun in the morning and behind my back in the late afternoon? I am so anxious to have this done so I can get to work painting. Leon, you did quite well. I'm proud of you. Now, get some lunch, and then come back. I'll tell you what I want next."

No Two People See the Same Thing

Emille and Luisa made their own lunch back at their apartment, cooking in the kitchen and eating at the table for two outside. They did not talk about what Monet had taught them in their morning lesson other than to agree not to have wine with lunch. The nice weather and lovely gardens gave them plenty to talk about.

When they'd finished their lunch, Luisa took the plates and silverware into the kitchen to wash them and put them away. Emille took a rag out to the table to clean it for the next couple, even if the next couple were her and Luisa or her and Jean. After cleaning up, they went back to their lesson with Monet. The sun warmed them as they strolled along the path, so they took time to study the trees, plants, and flowers along the way. Emille commented that there were many distractions because beauty could be seen everywhere. Luisa agreed.

They went to the easel and talked to each other about Monet's work. "When he does his quick glance and quick brushstrokes," Emille said, "I try to see what he saw, but it doesn't work."

Luisa pointed to Monet as he approached them.

"Any questions, ladies?"

Emille said, "I just told Luisa that I can't see what you see in the tree."

Luisa said, "Emille is right. You started with the tree, so I looked at it. But I've also acknowledged the horizon. I saw a bird land on the tree before lunch."

"Luisa, there is far too much attention on what you would not be painting at the moment. I don't want you to be narrow-minded," Monet said, laughing, "but I do want narrow vision."

"Did you teach Jean to have narrow vision?" Emille asked.

"Not at first, because he didn't ask questions. In time, of course, I did, and your time will come. For both of you ladies."

They both curtsied and resumed their seats on the green bench, pondering if Monet had just promised a series of lessons.

"When you go out to paint, try to forget what objects you have before you—a tree, a house, a person, or whatever," Monet said. "Merely think, *Here is a little square of blue, here an oblong of pink, and here a streak of yellow,* and paint it just as it looks to you—the exact color and shape—until it gives you your own naive impression of the scene before you. I'm sorry I didn't say that at the start of the lesson. No two people see the same thing when they look at an object. But in my theory, each artist needs to learn to see the basics of what is being painted. Here in this painting, see how the blue and yellow show where the sun shone this morning on different parts of the tree?"

The ladies stood up and walked closer to Monet's painting. Emille said, "Even the different thicknesses of the paint show the texture of the tree. The bark has a thickness that varies at different parts of the tree."

"Color can do many things in a painting if you know what you are doing. Do either of you ladies understand what I'm trying to teach you? It's a huge departure from what you've learned in the past. I start teaching here, asking you to watch me paint. Black and white make gray, don't they? They do, and different shades of gray define the object or scene I or any artist wants to paint. It's the same with colors. Okay, that is a lot to learn, and neither of you has grasped what I'm saying."

"Sir," Emille said, sitting back on her end of the bench, "I want to learn, as does Luisa." Luisa went back to her end of the bench.

"Fine. Watch me paint for a bit more, and then tomorrow we'll do something different."

Monet painted for a while, as he'd said, and then picked up his equipment and bid the ladies good evening.

The ladies simply sat on the bench, each still looking at the tree and then at an imaginary canvas. Finally, Emille got up and put her hands over her eyes. "I don't know how I am going to do what he says."

Luisa just nodded when she got up from the bench. They went

back to their apartment, not talking about painting or what they'd seen, though Luisa reminded Emille of the lesson with Degas in which each of them had started at a different point in the picture. Emille agreed with her and added, "That might have been what Monet meant."

The Dishes on the Menu

Monet put his painting and equipment in the studio and then went into the nearby woods. Instead of looking at the trees and sky, he focused on the ground. He had a cane with him so he could move the plants and leaves on the ground without having to bend over. In time, he found what he looked for: truffles, hidden on the ground, would be part of a nice dinner. The thought pleased him. The chef would be told to include truffles in the forthcoming menus, especially at dinner.

Every two weeks or so, Monet did his woods hunt, often getting enough truffles for two or even three meals. He discarded other mushrooms that, while tasty, didn't compare with truffles in his mind or his taste buds. He was known for fine cuisine and was in fact a wonderful fancier of food, which was almost as important to him as his gardening and perhaps even his painting. He worked closely with his chef, Marguerite, almost as much as with Jean and a few other gardeners.

When Monet returned from a trip to London, he had Marguerite find a recipe for Yorkshire pudding. She did find one, which involved combining egg, flour, rosemary, and freshly grated Gruyère cheese to make a batter and then cooking it in a cast-iron muffin pan. At first, Monet had her prepare the pudding every day, until Alice complained. They still had Yorkshire pudding at least once a week.

There was a bench—painted green, of course—partway into the woods. In the late afternoon, Jean often went to the bench, got comfortable, and watched the sunlight shine through the trees.

With the angle of the sun near dusk in the fall, before the leaves changed color, the sunlight highlighted some trees and branches but didn't shine on other parts of the woods. The angle changed, so his view of the sunlight changed as well.

Sometimes he hummed a tune when brightly lit branches went dark or dark leaves went bright. He tried to look at the parade of light and color as an artist would. Jean was an artist. He felt proud of finding that scene in Monet's gardens, especially since Monet didn't know about that display of nature in action.

Monet joined him there on the bench a few times but talked all the time about what Jean needed to learn to be a better artist. Jean listened because what Monet said was helpful, but then he couldn't concentrate on the sunlight.

Back at the boardinghouse where the ladies were staying, Luisa had a letter from her parents waiting for her. She waved it at Emille and then sat down at the table for two in the entry yard. "My parents are coming to Paris in a week. They want me to show them the best of Paris. They even want to go to the ballet."

"That's quite nice, Luisa. What are you going to do about their visit? And your lessons with Monet?"

"I'll take the lessons until the day before they are due to arrive. Then I'll go to Paris. They want a hotel room, so I won't need your room, even though you're staying here. Aren't you?"

"Luisa, would you mind if I went back to Paris with you? There are a few things I'd like to do. I'd also like the chance to meet your parents. And I would be happy to contact Degas. You know he's well liked at the ballet and paints some of the dancers. With and without their costumes."

"Don't tell my parents that. In fact, don't remind me of what he does with women. Oh, Emille, I'm sorry. I really like the way Degas teaches. I like his paintings, and when he keeps his hands and eyes to himself, I like him. I would like to have the same arrangement with him that Mary Cassatt has. It's all only about art."

"What about Monet? Your lessons here? Are you thinking of not coming back to Giverny? What about my lessons?"

"Emille, I will try to remember all the questions as I try to answer them. Monet is a wonderful painter with an outstanding vision of light and color. My lessons here will depend on what I can or can't arrange in Paris. I would love to come back to Giverny just to see how the gardens and the new pond look. I might even try to paint them. Your lessons are as important to you as mine are to me. I'm hoping we can come to a mutually acceptable decision, like we did when we picked out the tree to draw last visit."

"Thanks. We are friends who look out for each other. I'll have to think about where I will take my lessons and from whom. With you next to me. Let's go get dinner. In fact, let's have dinner at the hotel where we stayed."

They went to their room to change and then walked to the hotel, reminding each other about the dishes on the menu they wanted to try—with a bottle of wine.

How Are Your Students Doing?

Monet came into his kitchen with the truffles he had picked and gave them to his chef. "Marguerite, please cut some of these into thin slivers, and melt some cheese. Put the slivers into the cheese, and let it cool. We'll have it tomorrow. Oh, is dinner ready?"

Marguerite pointed to the stove and the pots ready to be served. She took the truffles and put them on a cutting board. The smell would delight her as she worked on them while Claude and Alice had dinner.

"Fine. Add a bottle of burgundy. We'll be ready soon." Monet went to sit with Alice on a couch in the living room.

"Claude, how are your students doing? I saw them walking toward the hotel a short while ago. Probably to eat there. It's a decent meal."

A server brought in the wine and two glasses and poured one

for Alice and the other for Monet. "To art," Alice said, raising her glass.

After they both had a sip of wine, Monet stood, walked around the room, and then sat back down where he had been sitting. "The two ladies have only known each other for maybe two weeks. They have an apartment with two bedrooms. When I went to Paris a few days ago, Degas told me he thought they were looking at a Boston marriage. You do know what that is, right?"

"I've heard that a Boston marriage is when two women live together so they can both focus on some work—like painting or medicine, for example."

"Right. Remember those two ladies from Boston? Ellen Hale and the other one? Gabrielle Clements? They studied here in Paris some of the time. Hale, I think, bought a place back near Boston, where they both live, and each has a studio there. That happened, oh, a dozen years ago. I think it is interesting that I've heard Hale is obsessed with painting in the morning and equally obsessed with gardening in the afternoon. They do more than paint together, some say. I have no idea, and I don't care."

"I don't remember them. Did you teach them?"

Marguerite called them to dinner then, so they went to the table in the dining room.

Monet said, "No, they wanted to paint at the Louvre—inside painting. Back then, a dozen years ago, I wasn't so emphatic about en plein air as I am now. Anyway, someone told me their place near Boston had studios for each of them, and that is where they paint. Inside.

"Have you noticed this chicken is really tasty? It has so much apple flavor. We use Granny Smith apples from Australia. We also have dry apple cider in the sauce."

Alice licked her lips to affirm what Monet had said. "Well, you are teaching these two ladies. Do you care if they have a Boston marriage?"

"Not in the least. And I'm not going to get involved with them.

Neither of them, not that I would under any circumstances. Jean may try to engage or seduce one of them. They stick together quite a bit, and Jean will be lucky to get close to either one." After taking a bite of chicken, he said, "Tell me this. Jean had two paintings at the Café de la Nouvelle Athénes. One I called a self-portrait where he looks like he's attracting women. Or ladies. Nice clothes and a welcoming smile. He admits he painted it to attract women. The other is one of a woman. He cleverly focused our eyes on her bosom. Emille bought the self-portrait. Luisa bought the portrait of the woman. Do you see any significance in their choices?"

"What do you mean? Are suggesting that Luisa likes women and not men? That Emille likes men? Both paintings sound just fine."

"They are decent paintings. Both won prizes at the Salon. As an aside, Jean is getting much better at painting en plein air. I have hopes for him."

"Claude, I've been thinking about the two ladies you are teaching now. Are they in a Boston marriage now? They live together, don't they? And here at the apartment house, they have the same room. I guess what I'm asking is this: What does our church say about that?"

Monet picked up his glass but didn't offer it to Alice for a toast. "I'm tempted to toast to God somehow or to what the ladies are doing. Seems like I need to take sides. You say the words."

Alice looked at him and then closed her eyes as she spoke. "Claude, we had an intimate relationship while you were married to Camille before she died. You were unfaithful, and I was unfaithful to my former husband and the father of my children. That is against our religion, though we don't do much with it. Remember, I couldn't get married to you until he died, according to the priest."

"Why bring that up? Did something happen?"

Alice pressed her lips together tightly. "I'm sorry I brought this up. I worry about things instead of ignoring them like you do." Then she said, "To us as we go through life together." They touched glasses and took a sip.

To Our Partnership in Art

Emille and Luisa were shown to a table in the hotel restaurant that had a nice view of the courtyard. They could see people coming into and leaving the hotel. The sun shone at an angle that focused down the path they had just walked. They took their time adjusting their skirts and getting settled in.

"It's like the sun is showing us the way home," Luisa said, "if we don't stay until midnight." Both ladies looked at the menu, and when the waiter came up to them, each asked for a glass of Shiraz wine rather than a bottle to share.

Emille studied the menu intently and then put it on the table. "I'm going with the pork rather than the salmon. I'm looking for some serious taste."

"Good idea. I'll try the same dish. Mushrooms should add some interesting flavor." Luisa put her menu down also.

The waiter came with their glasses of wine, took their orders, and left with the menus.

"A toast, Emille, to our partnership in art. And to us." They sipped their wine, set the glasses down, and looked at each other. "Is this true? Is there more to us than our partnership in art?"

"We are partners in art, Luisa, and maybe more. Depending."

"Depending on what? I said 'partnership in art' to make sure I focused on art, not any other partnership. Not a Boston marriage. Oh, I wish they called it a Boston partnership. It's so different from marriage." Luisa thought back to her life in her Philadelphia suburb. Bryn Mawr had strict rules for women's behavior and would not accept a Boston marriage. Could she live in Boston?

"Relax, Luisa. I'm not complaining, and I'm not offended. In fact, I want to consider our working together as artists as an affirmation of what we can do with a Boston marriage. Together. Your parents are coming to Paris. They will want to see our place. Will they accept that? Will they see that our partnership, our form of a chaste Boston marriage, is how we can make the climb to being good artists? Great artists! Isn't life about art? At least our lives?"

Her comments led to silence. The meal gave them plenty to do. They had lentil soup with kale and pearl onions; a fresh fruit salad; a tart; and, finally, the roast pork with cherries for the main course. When the waiter brought the pork, Luisa ordered a second glass of wine for each of them. They raved about the pork. When the waiter brought their wine, she asked him for the recipe. He said the owner of the restaurant insisted that all recipes were secret. "I can tell you the cherries are local. We were given this recipe from Marguerite—um, ah, Mr. Monet's chef. This pork dish is very tasty." He added that if they could make it at home they might never come back, or maybe another restaurant would use the recipe.

On their way out, they saw someone who appeared to be in charge. Emille said, "If I had a restaurant, I would hire one of your waiters and get all the recipes you have. We just wanted to enjoy the pork flavor when we get back to Paris."

The sun only faintly lit the path to their apartment, but they knew the way. When they reached the entry to their apartment, they found Jean at the table, sitting on a third chair. Three glasses sat on the table, and his glass held red wine. He rose, bowed to them, and then assisted them as they took their chairs. "Nice evening for a walk," he said.

"Yes, Jean, the walk with my friend Emille felt good. The pork dish tasted really good too." Luisa looked at the bottle of wine. "I think I'll have half a glass, if you don't mind, and then I'm going to bed."

After Luisa drank her half glass, she excused herself and went to her room. Emille drank a bit slower and then excused herself without any comment, even about art. Jean relaxed, thought briefly about going to Philadelphia, enjoyed the wine, and then went inside also.

They Turned to Face Each Other

When Luisa and Emille entered their apartment, they turned to face each other. Luisa put a towel over the mirror. "I want to get ready for bed. Back to back, no peeking, and no turning around until we're both ready. Get your nightgown."

After they had changed into their nightclothes, Emille sat on the chair by the desk. "I learned very early to be very modest. And I believe it is proper to be modest. That's why I am so shy about changing clothes with you in the room." She pulled her nightgown closer to herself. "I don't mean to imply you would do anything, but what do you think of when I change?" She frowned almost fiercely after asking that question.

Luisa went to the other chair, sat down, and crossed her arms. "I'm not implying anything either. I think that if we are going to be art partners—and I hope to heaven we will be—we need to get rid of some of our barriers but keep the important ones. We're each a young woman who wants to be an artist more than to be part of a life with a husband, children, maybe servants, and maybe housework. If I did that, I couldn't be an artist." Luisa paused and rubbed her arms. "The thing is, I don't want to be alone. I want to be with someone to talk to—about art mostly but also about what I see and what I think. I like to have someone to have a glass of wine or two with. I don't want to repeat absinthe."

Emille stood and walked over to Luisa. "I will get us a glass of wine." She went to her closet and came back with an open bottle and two glasses.

After they'd had one glass of wine each, Emille stood up again and held out her hand to help Luisa stand up. They faced each other and then shook hands. Neither lady made any motion for a hug. Then they stepped back, smiled, and said, "Good night. Sleep well."

You Both Bought It?

Part of the kitchen at the apartment house also served as the dining area, with three tables with three chairs each. The next morning, Luisa and Emille were eating omelets, when Jean came down the stairs. He waved and then sat down at a different table, taking a chair that let him see them. He had his sketchbook with him, as he'd started to draw a tree outside his bedroom window. He wanted to do more and expected to have some time that day to add to the drawing. He had been trying more and more to paint or sketch at every opportunity. He felt that the more art he attempted, the more it would be part of his life. Other artists further along than Jean had confirmed that they too believed they learned much by drawing all the time.

Emille got up and came over to his table. "Have you been sketching? May I see it?" She looked at the paper he held up. "That looks like the tree we can see from our room also. You are certainly an artist. I'm impressed."

Luisa also came over to see what he had drawn. "Nice work, Mr. Jean. And thanks for the idea. Do you think Mr. Monet would like to see my sketch of that tree?"

"Not today," he said, laughing, "but I'll show him mine and mention that the tree is outside our windows—our separate windows—and he'll suggest it if he wants to see it. That might be a really good way to be his student: letting him make suggestions.

Speaking of which, I need to hurry up with my breakfast because it's nearly time for the lesson today."

The two ladies cleared their table and went to find Monet. Jean took some pastry he could eat while walking and followed them out the door. He didn't try to catch up to them. Instead, he continued to look at his sketch of the tree.

As Jean walked to Monet's house, he thought about the ladies' reaction to his sketch. Both, he thought, had focused on their own opportunity to draw the tree, although both had given polite comments on his sketch. As an artist, he liked what they did. As a person interested in a relationship, not so much. He wondered if either of the ladies would have shown more interest in him without the other present. They stayed together so much he might never get the opportunity to find out.

When they got to Monet's house and studio, they didn't see Monet, so they relaxed. They sat on the green benches, as usual, with Jean alone, facing the ladies. A few minutes later, Monet came out of the studio, carrying two easels and canvases. "Good morning," he said to the three of them. "Jean, please go into the studio to get two palettes and the paint. I see you have your sketchbook, and I want to see what you have been doing. Or trying to do."

Jean hurried into the studio. He found the palettes and paint neatly stacked on a table. He didn't even have to put his sketchbook down to bring the supplies out.

"Follow me," Monet said, "and each of you ladies can carry an easel and canvas. You will need them for today's lesson. We're going to a field where there are some hay bales."

Memories of Jean's efforts for Monet on hay bales put his other thoughts aside.

"Mr. Monet," Luisa said as she tried to keep up with him, "Emille and I bought that haystack painting you had at the Café de la Nouvelle Athénes."

"You both bought it? How interesting." Monet slowed down when he saw that she struggled to keep up.

"We take turns having your painting, Mr. Monet."

Emille fell in line behind Luisa. They rounded a curve in the path and came upon a field with a dozen or so haystacks. Monet pointed to a spot, the ladies set up their easels, and then Jean gave each of them a palette and paint.

"Do you ladies see that haystack that has somehow been split in the middle? See how the sunlight looks different on the inside? That's your assignment. Paint that haystack. And keep in mind where the sun is as it changes. Get the light right first."

The ladies first looked at the hay bales. Emille used a brush to measure the dimensions of the split bale. Luisa began to paint without measuring. Both showed enthusiasm for the assignment.

Are You Going to Have a Ceremony?

Monet and Jean went back to the edge of the woods so they could sit on a fallen tree, which was not soft like a sofa. Monet asked to see the sketchbook and took his time to go over it.

"Jean, this is nice. My only question is this: Why does it seem like you are looking at it from above?"

"Claude, I see the tree from my bedroom window on the second floor of Madame Baudy's apartment house. My room is next door to the bedroom the ladies share."

Money looked over at them, leaning to see what progress they were making. "They can see the tree?"

"Yes, they can. Why?" Jean tried to keep from smiling.

"You can figure that out, Jean. I'll have them draw the same tree tonight. And I like how you led me to make the assignment. You do know me." Monet reached over and patted Jean on the shoulder.

"Claude, you give me too much credit. Well, maybe in this case, I simply told the ladies to not mention it, because if you liked an idea, then you would think of it. This is a lesson they needed to learn. Teachers have ideas. Students do what they are told."

Monet picked up Jean's sketchbook. "Do you think you can redraw this so it looks like you are on the ground? I mean without going outside to see it?"

"Claude, I look at that as a challenge. I'll try, and I'll show you how it turns out. By the way, are you going to have a ceremony when the water flows into the pond?"

"Ceremony? Why? The pond is for me." He stroked his beard. "Well, anyone who is here is welcome to watch. I think we'll open the water this afternoon."

"I'm absolutely sure all of us who had anything to do with the pond will want to be there."

"Fine. I'm going to check on the ladies to see if they did what I wanted." He patted Jean's shoulder again.

Jean stayed seated on the tree, trying to think of what painting or sketch he would try to make when the water started to flow into the pond. He didn't care about what would be done or how to open the flow, though that might make a big splash. He wanted to anticipate its beauty. Jean shook his head at his thoughts about selecting the picture he wanted to create. *I'm getting to be obsessed with art*, he thought, and he smiled.

Monet came back to the tree and sat down. He clenched both fists several times and then hit the tree they were sitting on, though nothing moved. "Jean, neither of those ladies heard me when I told them to pay attention to the light on the inside of the haystack that split open. One of them—Luisa, I think her name is—sketched the haystack all the way open so it divided like two smaller stacks. That way, the light is virtually the same as on the other stacks. Emille had the stack almost put back together, so only shadows can be seen in the spit. And guess what? Luisa's parents are coming to Paris soon, and both of the ladies are going back to Paris to meet them."

"Claude, isn't it typical for someone to meet one's partner's parents if some union is planned?"

They both groaned and then noticed the ladies were looking at them.

"Jean, you have a sense of humor. Let's go find the gardeners and get ready for filling the pond. The ladies can do what they want. I'm not impressed with this effort."

The Door Shot out into the Pond

It didn't take them long to find the gardeners. Leon had them clearing brush around the point where the pond would be connected to the river. Jean had helped them create a small path at the other end of the pond that would put the water back into the river. Some local government officials had sent Monet an order telling him not to grow strange plants because of fear they might contaminate or otherwise hurt other crops and plants. He ignored them, thinking of his friendships with top government people while also saying that if the water lilies, wisteria, and other plants worked elsewhere, why wouldn't they be fine in Giverny? That day, they would open the flow of water. Alice argued with her husband about ignoring the order, but he assured her of his political power. "Part of being a famous artist is getting to know important people. You know we've had Georges Clemenceau here for meals. Local officials will bow down to him."

Monet and Jean arrived at the site where the water would enter the pond. Monet quickly went to the spot. It looked like a dam of soil, grass, and some tiny branches. "Who is going to dig?" he asked. "Where is that door I told you to get?"

Leon pointed to the door and then had two gardeners put it on its side up against the river side of the ground, keeping the water out. Those gardeners then stood in the empty pond by the ground to be dug. They began filling buckets with the dirt, and other gardeners emptied the buckets where Monet told them to build the banks of the river up where it would flow into the pond. Jean felt proud of how efficiently the gardeners worked.

When the gardeners had most of the dirt removed, they got out of the pond. They each took one end of the door and tried to lift it. Water started to flow, and the door shot out into the pond along with a heavy flow of river water. Neither gardener felt pulled with the door into the pond. Monet looked pleased and then told Leon to have them start planting the water lilies as soon as the pond stabilized. Most of them sat down on the grass near the pond, resting in anticipation of the work ahead.

Monet then hurried along the side of the pond, which, in time, would become a path. He stopped when he got to the narrow point where he planned to put a bridge, making sure the water didn't erode the soil. Then he hurried to the end of the pond closest to his house. He had set up an easel and canvas earlier. Working quickly, as always, he sketched the flowing water as it came up to the shoreline where he stood.

Jean caught up to Monet and bent over the shore to put his hand in the water. Monet had been sketching, probably anticipating the bridge. "Jean, where is the plant? You're supposed to plant the water lilies, not just wash your hands." He went back to his sketching.

Jean began to ask him to explain his sketch but then heard the ladies approaching. Each carried her painting of the split haystack.

"Hi, Mr. Monet!" Emille shouted as the two ladies hurried up to him. "I changed my sketch. I felt so dumb when you came over to look at our work. I am dumb. I should have known you wanted the haystack drawn just like it was. So here." She thrust the canvas out to him. At the same time, Luisa put her canvas on the ground next to Emille so he could see that she too had drawn the split haystack as it was.

Somehow, Jean forgot to ask Monet about his sketch. He complimented both ladies on their efforts. Monet nodded approval and then said he truly felt pleased that they finally had done what he'd assigned. As he often did, he ignored them afterward, but they didn't walk away.

One Evening, He Felt Extra Tired

Monet continued to look at the two canvases and then at the two ladies. "Ladies, if you were Catholic and wanted to see the pope and you had to walk at times and ride a train at other times, consider where you would be at the shuttle you came here on. From your room to the shuttle, you could say you made some progress. But you would also have to admit that you had a long way to go compared to just getting to the shuttle. Well, in your paintings here, you both have made some progress, but you have a long way to go."

The ladies looked at the two canvases as if waiting for Monet to say more.

When he didn't, Emille walked in front of her canvas, looking Monet directly in the eye. "Sir, here is my palette. Please use it to show me how to go a little further. Like to the train station in Vernon or even the Saint-Lazare station in Paris. It's still a long way to go to see the pope."

Monet looked at Emille and then at Luisa, who looked down at the ground to avoid his eyes. When he looked at Jean, Monet grinned. "She has the right idea. Here, Emille. I'll take the palette. See here how the top of the haystack has bright spots and shadows? It needs more." He quickly added the pattern of light and dark. "The sides of the haystack are dull. Put some light and shadow here." He gave the haystack a few more quick strokes with the brush. "Both of you should practice this. And that's all for today."

The ladies stared at Emille's painting, each expressing amazement at the change his few brushstrokes had made to the haystack. His answer to her question had taught them a lot.

Monet went back up the path to the inlet. Jean followed, bringing his sketchbook to capture some changes in the pond now that it had water. He stopped at one point, while Monet kept walking. Jean's lesson for the day had ended too.

The next few days, they settled into routines after the pond had filled. Jean worked partly on planting, having sessions with Monet to discuss his garden plans. He also painted the tree he could see from his room's window. Using perspective, Monet helped Jean lower the point of view. He should have thought of that, he realized.

Jean didn't see Emille or Luisa much, though the three of them established a routine of sharing an evening bottle of red wine outside the apartment house. They even took turns selecting and buying the wine. They showed him the sketches they'd made of the tree behind the building. Luisa had drawn it from her bedroom window and had it looking level. How did she know to do that? She told him she'd just imagined herself down on the ground and drawn what she imagined seeing. Emille had gone outside to draw her sketch. He complimented them both and added that each of them had her own way of drawing, and both were successful. Jean wasn't certain if Monet would think so.

One evening, Jean felt extra tired from the planting he had been doing that day. He put his chair away and excused himself. That didn't bother the ladies. They said they would be happy to finish the wine.

Are People like That?

After Jean left, Luisa asked Emille if she had heard that opposites attracted. "One of the gardeners showed me a magnet. He called one end the north pole and the other the south pole. He had another magnet, and he pointed to the same two poles. He then moved the magnets to be in contact. When the two north or two south ends of both magnets were put in contact, nothing happened. But when a north pole on one contacted the south pole on the other, they stuck together solidly. Are people like that?"

"People aren't magnets. I don't know if people have north or south poles." Emille shook her head as if she could wipe the poles idea from her mind. "Are you saying that because a man and a woman are opposite genders, that's why they are attracted to each other? I don't think that if they are opposite in, say, disposition or hobbies or whatever that would help their marriage. They'd just go their separate ways."

"Emille, you are probably right, I think. People aren't magnets. But how does that work for you and, say, Jean?"

"Jean? What do you mean?"

Luisa took a sip from her glass of wine. "I don't know. I thought about the magnets and thought about men. I'm not attracted to men at all. Let's finish our wine and go inside."

"Not right away, Luisa. What did you mean about me and Jean? He's a man, and both of us are women. But you say you aren't attracted to men. If I am at least pleased to be with handsome men, like Jean perhaps, does that mean you and I are opposite poles like your magnets? Are you attracted to me? I hope not." She leaned away as she spoke.

"Emille, no, of course not." Luisa blushed. "Not that way for sure. Look, we are painting partners. That is all we've been, and that's all we will be. Being painting partners is helping both of us to become better painters, in part because we can be so focused on our art. We're artists. Like Mary Cassatt. I guess I just wondered if you were attracted to Jean and I would lose my painting partner."

"You don't have another bottle of wine, do you? We're doing fine, and in two days, we'll be back in Paris. Let's just relax and talk about the lesson today."

"You are reading my mind, Emille. I'll go get the wine. We will just relax."

The wine became all they talked about for a while. Then Emille sighed and said, "What did you think about what Mr. Monet said about his conversation with Degas about God?"

"I've had some trouble thinking it through. Monet said God created the outside, and that's why we should paint en plein air. People created inside, not God. Then Degas replied that God lives in the hearts of people, who live inside, so God created inside. Jean says they argue like that all the time. I'm not convinced."

"Neither am I," Luisa replied.

They spent some time finishing the wine and then cleaned up and went to their room.

As Well as What?

Their lives at Giverny the next day had no surprises other than when Monet told Jean to go to Paris when the ladies went. "Take your tree painting, and find a buyer. If you're going to be successful, especially enough to live as an artist and gardener on your own, you need to sell your art. And while you ride the train and look out the window, try to figure out what specific objects or scenes you are going to be known for. I did hay bales and the cathedral in Rouen. I'm planning to paint the pond if you gardeners ever get the water lilies planted. Relax. I know you are working as hard as you can. I also affirm your work as a painter along with the planting."

What could Jean say to that? He planted for a while and then touched up the painting of the tree so it would be dry when he took it to Paris tomorrow. He also bought a bottle of champagne to share with the ladies that night.

Monet also invited Jean to join him and his wife, Alice, for dinner in his home. "It's not a goodbye dinner, just a chance to be social for a while. You are coming back, aren't you?"

Jean assured him that his place was at Giverny. At dinner, he said he treasured the opportunities to learn to paint and garden more than anything else.

"Jean," Monet said in reply, "I'm good for nothing except painting and gardening."

Alice looked at Jean with a smile.

Jean said, "I'm sure she easily could find something else you're good at. Right, Alice?"

"He does select the colors here in the house quite artistically, but maybe that's part of his painting goodness. He decides on our menus as well as—"

"As well as what?" Monet asked his wife, interrupting her. They both acted as if Jean had disappeared from the room. "Are you suggesting anything?" All three of them laughed and went back to eating the Claude-created cuisine.

Later, Jean sat at the table in the sand court with the ladies. He popped the cork on the champagne and filled the flutes. He had just set the bottle on the table, when Emille stood up, picked up her glass, and said, "This is a toast to you, Mr. Jean, for helping Luisa and me work with Mr. Monet as his students. To you, Mr. Jean."

He had stood up as she started to speak. The three touched their flutes and then took a sip. He bowed to Emille and Luisa. It occurred to him to try to hug each of them, but Emille sat down after pulling her chair a bit away from him. "Mr. Jean, you are also a nice, polite gentleman. I will call you Jean."

"Thank you, Emille. And Luisa. It is fascinating to watch you both work extremely hard to be artists. You have different ways, but both of you are making wonderful progress. It's not my doing. It's you. Congratulations."

They all agreed the champagne tasted good.

Once Again, He Thought of a Hug

After breakfast the next morning, Jean took his painting and some things to the shuttle stop. The ladies were waiting there with all their luggage and painting gear. "Do you really need everything?" he asked. "It looks like you have everything you brought here. Or are you not coming back maybe?"

Emille came over to him and said, "Are you a mind reader? I can't say for sure what we will be doing. Not coming back is one possible item on our agenda."

"Have you told Mr. Monet? If not, here's your chance. He's coming now."

The ladies turned quickly to see him walking toward them,

and he waved. Emille grabbed Jean's arm. "Jean, help us. We don't want a scene."

He stepped away and started walking toward Monet. "I'll try."

When he reached him, they shook hands.

"Jean, I wanted to see your painting before you left for Paris. Do you have it?"

"Yes, Claude. I'll get it."

"That's okay. I'll walk with you. It will give me a chance to say goodbye to my lady students. Looks like they have all their stuff. Aren't they coming back?"

"They said they needed their stuff because some of it isn't necessary here. They're both nervous about Luisa's parents."

When he reached the ladies, Monet pleasantly greeted them and then focused on Jean's painting. His comments on the effort Jean had made to softly wrap shadows on the trunk of the tree were, Jean thought, intended for the ladies more than for him. Most of what Monet said repeated all the comments he'd told Jean at the studio. When Monet had finished, he thanked Jean, wished him good luck with a sale, and saluted the ladies. When Monet had walked a decent distance from them, the ladies thanked Jean profusely. Once again, he thought of a hug but didn't try for one, not wanting a rejection.

The shuttle arrived a few moments after Monet left them. As usual, Jean rode facing backward, and the women sat facing forward. Once they boarded the train to Paris, the ladies piled their stuff on the seats next to them, leaving no room for him, so he sat facing them, next to the window so he could look out. He wanted to think about Monet's suggestion that he find an object or objects outside to concentrate on, as Monet had with hay bales and the Rouen cathedral. The streets of Montmartre were the only thing that came readily to his mind. Trees had been primary in his work with Monet, and the painting he'd sold had garnered significant interest from those passing by his spot in the park. He couldn't picture himself painting that same tree over and over.

Monet painted the same hay bale or cathedral at different times of day to show the effects of the sun at different angles. He didn't plan to do that. As he said that to himself, a branch from a tree near the train brushed his hand, which he had put on the open window. He laughed out loud, and the ladies asked why he laughed. He said, "Mother Nature is joking with me."

13

He Made a Mental Journey

W hen Jean got to Paris, he went back to the open land near the Louvre, where he'd sold his other painting. He set up his easel, put the painting on it, and waited. Occasionally, someone would come up to look more closely at the painting. Several asked if Monet had painted that piece of art, and Jean again affirmed in his mind that many of those passing by knew much about art. One time, a woman with many pieces of jewelry came up and leaned forward to see the signature. She wore a pendant watch that swung away from her as she leaned. He asked, "Is that an enamel watch?"

"Yes. It's from Paris, but the movement is Swiss. A friend gave it to me."

Now maybe he had an answer to a question he'd had for years: a mistress called her lover a friend. "Maybe he will buy this painting for you."

"He has already bought me a Monet. But this is also nice." She went on her way.

Others stopped to look at his canvas, sometimes commenting. When no one came up to the painting, he continued to think about what his hay bale or cathedral would be. He looked at the few trees in sight, finding no interest in painting them. Trees were not his cathedral. That did suggest something, however, and he would later consider a building there in Paris, where there were many wonderful buildings, though they were not as tall as Monet's cathedral. Monet's advice to find something made a lot of sense, especially for Monet because the later hay bales sold for more than the first few because others had to have one. That led Jean to the debate between inside and outside painting. Degas or Monet?

Jean made a mental journey up the road in Montmartre, which had been his first thought of what he would paint many times. Monet painted the same thing, a hay bale or a cathedral, but nothing in the whole Montmartre district stood out in Jean's mind. Perhaps painting different parts of Montmartre would be a compromise—en plein air but also focusing on different scenes in the district.

Degas would not care what he did, especially if he painted it outdoors. Monet wouldn't be satisfied that his work supported en plein air, especially if he had different subjects. On the one hand, Degas painted ballet dancers, including some without their clothes. That had an appeal. Monet had painted landscapes, trees, sea scenes, and even the Saint-Lazare train station in Paris. That painting showed the same effect of the sun.

Jean found himself smiling at the thought of each painting having the subject that appealed to him at that moment, or at least what he found to be an appropriate scene. He tried to think of other artists who focused on one object or scene. Maybe if he saw her again, he thought, he would do a portrait of the lady with the enamel pendant watch—or without it.

His thoughts were occasionally interrupted by passersby wanting a closer look at his painting. When they left without buying it, he affirmed that trees would not be his hay bale or cathedral. But what would be?

Father, It's about Art

Luisa's parents arrived in Paris in the morning. Luisa and Emille went to the dock to greet them and get a carriage to take them to their hotel. Luisa also helped them register at the hotel they had selected, even though the desk clerk spoke English. Her father wore tan slacks, black shoes, a white shirt, and a loose bow tie under a lengthy black coat that was open to near the end of his ribs and extended halfway down his thighs. As soon as Luisa introduced Emille to him, Emille said he truly looked like a Parisian. She couldn't tell if he saw that as a compliment. Luisa's mother wore a dress that Luisa said looked just like what she'd worn the day she met Emille.

After her parents put their luggage in their room, the four of them had a nice lunch at the hotel. All had the spinach soufflé at Luisa's suggestion because she and Emille had eaten it at Café de la Nouvelle Athénes. Luisa described millas, the appetizer they'd had at the cafe, and how the cooks made it from cornmeal. Her father asked her to describe the café, which she did in detail, leaving out the absinthe incident but naming some of the famous artists they'd met.

Emille interrupted her, saying they had purchased three paintings at the café. "We pooled our money to buy a Monet painting of a haystack. We've also had some lessons from him at this place named Giverny, about an hour away by train. Each of us has a painting by Jean Forgeron, whom we met at Monet's gardens. He paints more like Monet now, but the ones we bought are works he did prior to Monet's influence."

Her mother asked, "Where do you stay in Giverny? Do you have separate rooms like at your apartment?"

"Emille and I have separate beds in one room, Mother. But we're not sure we are going back to Mr. Monet."

"And why is that, dear daughter?" her father asked.

"Father, it's about art. Mr. Monet insists we paint outdoors. The French call it en plein air." She spelled it for him. "Mr. Degas sometimes has us paint in the Louvre, copying some of the greatest painters. So far at the museum, we've only copied a painting of the holy family. Other times, we're at his studio. His focus is on painting inside."

"Luisa is right. There is a big debate about inside and outside paintings. When artists are at the café, the arguments get loud, we have learned. The painter we each bought a painting from, Jean, who is good, is struggling to decide which way he'll go. Speaking of *go*, is it time, Luisa, to go to the Louvre?"

"As the gentleman of this group, I would be pleased to escort you to the Louvre," Luisa's father said, "but one of you artistic young ladies will have to decide which paintings we will enjoy."

"Father, we will show you some of the best art in the world. We will show you the inside and outside paintings that are fueling the debate some are having—and some have resolved, like Degas and Monet."

"Yes, Mr. Slagle, it would be an honor to have you escort us," Emille said.

"Then let us depart. Do we walk? Or should we have a carriage? Maybe a carriage is best since we will be walking in the museum." That was what they chose.

Two horses pulled the carriage, with the rider sitting at the front. He had a whip and a brake at his disposal. There were two seats inside, facing each other, which were as wide as the carriage. Emille looked at Luisa and then pointed to the seat facing the direction of travel. Luisa's mother moved in front of the two ladies and climbed into the carriage. She said, "I think the forward-facing seat will give your father and me a better view of the part of Paris we will see."

Emille kept her eyes closed the whole time in the carriage.

Let's Move On to Something More Moral

Emille laughed to herself when the foursome came to Rembrandt's painting titled *Bathsheba at Her Bath*. As she expected, Mr. Slagle immediately frowned at Bathsheba, who was naked and not concerned about who might see the painting. Bathsheba also seemed unconcerned that someone had started to wash her feet. He turned his back to the painting and glared at Luisa, who continued to look at it. "Luisa, there is no place for a painting that immoral."

"Father, his wife served as the model, though I don't know which one. Besides, it is a painting of an ancient, oh, famous woman named Bathsheba. In any case, Emille and I have not done any painting of nudes."

"I should hope not. Did he have two wives at one time?"

"No, Father. His first wife died, and quite a few years later, he married his second wife. She too died, of the plague. Rembrandt is known as a truly great artist, but he had a sad life outside of painting."

"Let's move on to something more moral."

The statue of Venus de Milo was the next famous art object they viewed. "Another naked woman," Luisa's father said as he turned his back on the statue. "The French must be immoral themselves to have a museum full of these things."

"Father, it is a statue made by a Greek artist maybe hundreds of years before Christ."

"Before Christ? No wonder her arms are gone." No one laughed at his joke.

Most of the artwork on display did not upset Luisa's father. He saluted the painting by Eugène Delacroix titled *Liberty Leading the People*. "Daughter, this painting speaks to me. I know the French had a revolution, as did the United States. Liberty is something I hold close to my heart."

Luisa's mother, Ruth, had not said anything in the Louvre, looking at each painting with her arms folded and no expression on her face. Now she said, "Edward, this is liberty, and it is close to my heart also. I am proud of you for saluting this painting." They moved on.

"Father, Mother, in this room is the painting Emille and I copied when we were students of Edgar Degas. It's Rembrandt's *The Holy Family*. Very moral. Oh, look. Mr. Degas is here. Come see the painting we copied and meet Mr. Degas."

Degas turned to meet the two ladies and then saw a more mature couple with them. As they approached, he asked his student to keep working and then walked up to greet them. "Emille, Luisa, it is a pleasure to see you again. May I have the honor of meeting this distinguished couple with you? Let's go over here so we don't disturb my student."

Luisa put her finger to her mouth, telling Emille to be silent, when they stopped a distance from his student. "Mr. Degas, it is my pleasure to introduce you to my father, Mr. Edward Slagle, and my mother, Mrs. Ruth Slagle. They have been looking forward to meeting you."

"Good afternoon, Mr. and Mrs. Slagle. It is my pleasure."

Mr. Slagle walked up to Degas and extended his hand. "I have a friend in Philadelphia who admires your teaching of his daughter, Mary Cassatt."

Luisa screamed at her father, "You know Mary Cassatt's father? Why didn't you tell me? I want to talk to her."

"Daughter, don't shout. Relax, Luisa. I want to compliment Mr. Degas on his fine relationship with his very famous student. She is highly regarded in America." He smoothed the collar on his black coat.

"Thank you, Mr. Slagle. Mary Cassatt is highly regarded in France as well. I have been hoping these two ladies might also be highly regarded someday. They both have the talent. I don't compare my students, which is why I say they both have talent. And it is true."

Degas and the Slagles talked for a while as Emille tried to calm Luisa's frustration with her father, and then Degas said he had to get back to his student. They agreed to visit Degas at his studio and then went on to see more art.

Oh, Father, I Am Just Teasing Her

After their time in the Louvre, Luisa's mother sat on a bench, breathing a bit heavily. She asked her daughter where they were going next. Luisa told her they would be going to the Café de la

Nouvelle Athénes. Emille asked why Luisa wanted her parents to go there. She replied that the café often hosted famous artists as well as authors who came together to talk about the art world. "If my parents can see and even be introduced to Cézanne, Pissarro, or maybe Renoir, they will be the envy of family and friends back home. It will also help them understand more what I—and you, of course—experience in addition to actual painting. Plus, it's a nice place, and we can have some wine, if Father would enjoy that."

He pleasantly nodded an affirmation.

"I just hope Camille's shift is over and she's gone," Emille said.

"Emille, why do you say that? Are you jealous of Camille?"

"Why would Emille be jealous, Luisa? What do you mean?" her father asked.

"Oh, Father, I was just teasing her. Camille is a waitress who has introduced us to things, like food. The soufflé we had at lunch is like one she served us at the café. She described the millas she also served us. Plus, she knows all the artists, and they talk to her. That's all I meant."

Emille laughed. "The only thing I would be jealous of is if you were a better painter than I am. And you are not. Not a better painter but an equal. Remember, we are painting partners. Aren't we?"

Luisa stood between Emille and her father. She frowned at her painting partner, who laughed at her.

Luisa's mother reached out to her. "Darling, let's just go to the café and enjoy some wine and maybe a meal. Whom we meet isn't important. We have you and your painting partner."

Mr. Slagle escorted them out through the lovely front entrance of the Louvre to a carriage to go to the café. The two ladies often walked to or from the museum and the café, but Luisa's mother had walked enough and felt worn out.

When they arrived at the café, Luisa and Emille pulled two tables together and seated her parents in chairs with a view of the café. The ladies would watch the entrance for famous artists.

The waitress, Camille, came up to the table. "Welcome to our café," she said. "Luisa and Emille, it is nice to see you again. And you, sir and madam, are also quite welcome. Are you going to have dinner? Should I recite the menu?"

"One moment, Camille. Father, do you think some red wine first would be appropriate? Mother?"

"We have other drinks also," Camille said.

"Red wine," her father said. "Pinot noir."

Camille went to get the wine. Luisa thanked her father, who pretended to wipe his brow. Then he reached over and patted Luisa's arm.

When Camille came back with a bottle of pinot noir, Luisa asked her when her shift ended. Emille laughed and pointed to an area at the table where another chair would fit. Luisa also pointed to the area and suggested Camille join their table. Emille stood, pointed to her chair, and said, "I think I'm going for a walk in the sun. It is a fine idea that Camille should join you. She knows very much about Paris as well as the artists who patronize this lovely café."

Maybe I'll Paint One

Emille ignored Luisa's father when he told her to stay. She just smiled, patted Luisa on her shoulder, and walked out. She thought about Luisa and Camille and how her father would more easily understand Luisa's and her Boston marriage than one between his daughter and a waitress. She could also affirm her own good morals.

As she walked toward her apartment, she saw several couples walking along. They seemed content to be with each other. The women wore fancy dresses, including a woman who wore a dress with buttons from her neck down to the hem of her skirt. One couple had a little dog on a leash. As they walked past Emille, she looked at the dog and smiled. It tried to jump up onto her skirt. "That's a pretty pet," she said.

The gentleman took off his hat to greet her and then loosened the leash, saying in English, "This is a Papillon. He is a lap dog, and they are quite popular in France. Do you know the breed?"

Emille felt its ears. "No, unfortunately, I don't. I'm from Philadelphia."

The lady reached down and petted her dog. "Our Papillon is named Coco. *Papillon* is French for 'butterfly.' His ears look quite like a butterfly. Royalty had them before the revolution. Marie Antoinette had Papillons that I've heard were with her to the end. She had a Papillon named Coco that lived, I read, to twenty-two years of age. That many years is remarkable for a dog. If you are interested, there is a building here in Paris named Papillon House that you can visit."

Emille got up and bowed to the couple. "Thank you for letting me pet your beautiful little guy. Your Papillon. Maybe I will paint one."

"Oh, are you an artist?" The woman quickly picked up Coco and held him in her arms. Coco had his mouth open, panting. "Do you have a studio? Would you like to paint Coco?"

Emille stepped back and then came forward to pet Coco. "You are a lovely couple. Very dignified. I think you should have a portrait of you in your fine clothing, with one of you holding Coco. I am an art student studying with Degas and Monet. I have a friend who is a very competent artist. I will talk with him. He would do a great job. I have one of his paintings, and he is becoming quite popular. How can I get in touch with you?"

"Here is my card," the man said, handing it to her. "Please send a messenger, or feel free to come yourself. Just come when you are ready to have your friend paint our portrait. With Coco, of course. And tell me the cost when you stop by. It has been a pleasure meeting you."

Emille looked at his card. "It has been my pleasure, Mr. Berléal.

"Please call me Charles. And my wife's name is Suzanne." He tipped his hat, and then the couple walked away with Coco bouncing along on the leash.

Emille continued her walk and said out loud, "How do I find Jean?"

Another couple looked at her, as if to identify her as an American. Emille affirmed in her mind that Jean was capable of painting a portrait of the couple and their Papillon. She had his self-portrait. She also decided she would paint the Papillon Coco. She stopped at a bench and pulled out her sketch pad. Starting with the narrow nose, she drew what she remembered of Coco. A front view, the sketch clearly showed the butterfly ears and hair. She decided she would go back to the café that night to find Jean.

I Have a Proposition for You

Eventually, as Jean waited for someone to show serious interest in his painting, he mostly relaxed. The park always had art fanciers walking to and from the Louvre, as well as other traffic. Some simply wanted to be in a park. He had his sketch pad and enjoyed drawing some of the lovely ladies who walked by. Guys, even those escorting lovely ladies, did not make his sketches.

He almost dropped his sketchbook when he saw the lady with the emerald watch coming back with a gentleman in tow. He noted that she had the same dress on, with just a glimpse of herself showing. Her skirt whirled as she practically left the gentleman behind. Would Jean be lucky?

She came up to him—or, rather, to the painting as she ignored him. While he normally didn't let people touch his paintings, he said nothing as she gently stroked the trunk of the tree. She looked up at him. "Is this really yours? It has the texture of my Monet. I have a seascape by him."

Jean smiled. "I painted this at his gardens in Giverny. He did give me a number of suggestions." He stood up and nodded to the gentleman. She continued to examine the painting from every angle.

The gentleman walked up. "How much for the painting? It is quite like Monet's work. I like your work."

Jean told him, and he offered less but still more than Jean's bottom line for the painting. Jean said, "I have a lot of time invested in this painting. Mr. Monet even approved the squirrel."

The man added ten francs to the price, and Jean held out his hand. The man paid him and then told the lady he would carry the painting to her apartment. Jean smiled and put the money in his pocket. He looked around and then shook his head in disbelief when he saw Emille coming toward him, walking fast. He wondered how she'd known where to find him.

"Jean," she said, puffing a bit from walking fast. "Did that man buy your painting? The one of the tree? I really liked it."

"His lady friend liked it also. He bought it for her. And I got a fair price. Sit on the bench. Why were you hurrying? Is everything okay?"

She looked at the bench, sat down, and tried to compose herself, smoothing her skirt. "I started to hurry, as you call it, when I saw them leave with the painting. Everything is fine, at least as far as I know. Luisa took her parents to Café de la Nouvelle Athénes for a meal. I left. And I have a proposition for you."

"I like that idea."

"Jean, be serious. I met a couple on my walk here from the café. They had a cute little dog. A papillon. Do you know the breed?"

"Yes, I grew up with one. Lots of fun to play with, especially when they get the zooms." He waved his hands to exaggerate the zoom. "Why?"

"I told them I wanted to paint the dog. Coco is his name. Same as Marie Antoinette's dog."

"I know all about that. Her Coco lived twenty-two years, which is long even for papillons. What is your proposition?"

"When I said I studied to be an artist, they asked me if I did portraits. I said no but told them I know a good artist who would be great for their portrait. The gentleman gave me his card. You can paint their portrait. You can keep the money for it too. I want to paint their papillon, Coco. He is so cute and friendly."

He sat down on the bench, sitting as far away from her as he could. She didn't move farther away, as she usually did. He thought about painting a portrait. He could do it, he decided. "I assume the papillon will be in the painting. I'll have to ask Degas how much to charge. And maybe how many hours it will take me to complete it. A couple nicely dressed with the dog?"

"I'll wait to contact him then. He said he wanted a price when I set up a date."

"Emille, that's fine. Plus, I expect to see Degas at the café tonight. Let's try to both sit next to him."

"On either side of him? Or together? And that's not a proposition either."

I Do Know Something
about Portraits

E mille went home, hoping to talk with Luisa, only to find a note from her saying her mother felt tired, and she and her father were going to sit in the lobby of their hotel to talk about life. Luisa added that she doubted she would be at the café that night.

When Luisa and her parents entered their hotel, her father took her mother up to their room after telling Luisa to wait for him. She took a seat and looked at the lobby, grateful for the chance to do so.

The hotel lobby seemed to lift everyone up, with huge arches forming a ceiling of alternating green stripes and white-patterned surfaces. The arches joined the wall on the left as one entered, while the arches on the wall to the right ended as windows. Streetlamps, each with a cluster of four white lamps, marked the carpeted path to the desk where one registered or paid one's bill. Wooden chairs with red cushions grouped around wooden tables gave people a place to gather for conversation or get away from the talk of others. She wondered if royalty felt the way she did.

Luisa eased back and then sat up when her father approached her.

"Your mother is resting now, probably already asleep. I like the table you chose."

"Father, it is where I can see most of the beauty and majesty. You chose well too. I have never been in such a nice hotel."

"Now, my dear daughter, tell me about yourself. About your relationship with Emille. And with our waitress tonight." He leaned forward and gestured for her to speak.

"Father, Emille and I are painting partners. Both of us want to be as good as Mary Cassatt, and both of us have a long way to go to achieve that. That's all. As far as the waitress, she is just a waitress. Why do you ask?"

Her father stood up, leaned back and forth, and then walked around a streetlight next to their table and chairs. When he again stood in front of her, he put his hands in his pants pockets and then said, "Back in Bryn Mawr, you had many lady friends and no boyfriends. Your mother and I have observed that you don't seem interested in males."

Luisa stood up. "I'm a solid Episcopalian, and I practice my faith. It is a sin for a woman to engage with a man. People here in France say that I am very proper. They say that about Emille also. Paris has many Catholics who honor their faith, in spite of what you see on the streets. I'm not going to be like those women."

"Those women, as you call them, are prostitutes who seek to have men pay them for what they do to them. Not with other women. I accept what you say about yourself and am pleased that your faith has brought you to be proper. It is time for us to retire. Can you get to your apartment alone safely?" He moved toward her, opening his arms to hug her.

Luisa went sideways into his arms. "Good night, Father. I will be safe going home." She left him as he stood, not looking back at him.

Back in the apartment, Emille felt pleased that Luisa had decided not to bring her parents to the café that night. She rested in her bedroom until it was time to go to the café. She changed her dress, shaking out the wrinkles. She didn't walk in a hurry, expecting Jean to make things happen his way. When she reached the door to the café, he called to her to come across the street to a place where they could watch for Degas. When the artist arrived, Jean led Emille in behind him, gently positioned her on one side of Degas, and took the other side. Emille sat up as tall as she could.

"Well, what have we here?" Degas said as he sat at one of the tables the other artists had pulled together. "Do I see a relationship developing?" He looked at Emille with a smile.

"Edgar, that isn't happening. What is happening is that Emille has made an acquaintance with a couple who have a papillon. Named Coco, of course. The couple want me to paint their portrait. I thought I'd get some advice from you. Or anyone else at the tables."

Pissarro nodded and pointed to Degas.

"Jean, I hope this works out for you," Degas said. "How much do you know about portrait painting? Have you seen *Portrait of Madame X*? John Singer Sargent painted it—I think in 1884— and lost all of his clients because of the controversy. The off-the-shoulder dress strap pushed a lot of us to complain. Madame X—or, really, Madame Pierre Gautreau—did not commission that painting. Sargent went to England, even though he is an American."

As she listened, Emille made sure her shoulders were properly covered.

"Edgar," Jean said, "this will be a portrait of a proper and well-dressed couple with their papillon. Nothing sexy and nothing suggestive of anything other than pride in their pet. I do know something about portraits. Those two that hung here, of that lovely and fully clothed woman and my self-portrait, were done right. I know that one starts with the outside of a person's head, not inside. The opposite of our debate on painting in general. Emille tried to sketch the papillon but started with the nose instead of the entire head. It didn't work. Sorry, Emille."

"Jean, I remember those paintings of yours," Degas said. "Yes, they were good. And yes, the artist starts on the outside, like you described. Accept the commission. And thank Emille."

"Thank you, Edgar. Please tell me how much I should charge and estimate how long it will take for me to paint it. But don't say how much out loud. Write the numbers on this piece of paper." Jean put a sheet from a notebook in front of Degas, who used a charcoal stick to write the amount.

The rest of the evening was fine. Jean had a bottle of cabernet sauvignon and shared it with Emille. When Degas offered to trade chairs with her so she could sit next to Jean, she declined. Jean decided he would walk her home. They finished the wine and enjoyed listening to the other artists discuss the up-and-coming Salon. Emille stood up, thanked Degas, and nodded to the other artists. Jean said he wanted to be a gentleman and escort her home. Degas laughed when he made a comment about absinthe, which caused Emille to blush. Emille tried to laugh until they got outside the café; then she stepped away from Jean.

I Know You Like Men

On the walk to her apartment, Emille stayed away from Jean, moving ahead of or behind him if he came close to her. He had his hands in his pants pockets, which gave her some comfort. She felt nervous when they approached her apartment building. She remembered he'd treated her fine the last time he'd walked her home, after the disaster of seeing Degas painting a nude woman. *But will he try to kiss me? Would I resist? I don't know what to do.* Fortunately, he took hold of her elbow as they came to the door. He stepped forward, pulling the door open while staying to one side so she could enter the building without encountering him. She blushed and then said she looked forward to reporting to the couple about the portrait.

When she got into her apartment, she locked the door and then went directly to her bedroom, not looking to see if Luisa had come home to her own bedroom. She stood in front of the self-portrait of Jean she had hung on the wall and then quickly got in bed, replaying the day's events in her mind. It occurred to her she might be thinking of having Jean in bed with her. She decided she would do better with him hanging on the wall.

The next morning, she watched the sunlight coming through the curtained window. She went about getting ready for the day. When she went into the main room, planning to go to the bathroom down the hall, she saw Luisa, who was also ready to go down the hall.

They talked for a bit, and then Emille went first, hurrying, anxious to talk more with Luisa. Both ladies were efficient and soon were ready for breakfast.

Their conversation at the nearby café felt intense to both ladies. Luisa told Emille her mother had felt uncomfortable, not because of the food at Café de la Nouvelle Athénes. She'd gone straight to bed when they reached their hotel room. Luisa didn't go into what she and her father had discussed other than to say her father had wanted to know more about Emille as well as what kind of relationship the two of them had. He'd focused his comments on people he knew in Pennsylvania, New Jersey, and Massachusetts, particularly in Boston.

"Luisa, did he mention Boston marriages?"

"Not specifically. He talked about Mary Cassatt, who has no relationship with a man or a woman, and two women who live together but are artists and have separate studios as well as separate rooms in a house with others as well. I think those were his examples of relationships he could accept."

Emille replied that in her mind, as of now, their relationship remained solely about painting. She described her time walking home with Jean, when she'd wondered if and almost feared he would try to kiss her good night. "He didn't," she quickly added, and then she said that she did feel an attraction to him. "My point, Luisa, is that I have never wondered if you were going to kiss me. I am a person who is attracted to men."

Luisa fussed with her food and then smiled. "I know you like men. I know you like Jean. Nothing wrong with that if you stay careful. So are you asking me who I like?"

Emille also fussed with her breakfast and then frowned. "I see that you are attracted to other women. I'm not saying it is bad at all. We are who we are. But you and I should not go beyond who and where we are now. Not even as far as the absinthe disaster. I say 'should not' because each of us has the right to make our own decisions. And we must respect the other's right to make her own decisions about relationships. If I brought Jean to my bedroom, which I absolutely do not intend to do, it is none of your business. The same if you brought Camille to your bedroom—it is none of my business. But I think we should be very careful. You do remember the absinthe disaster, when we slept together, though we did nothing improper."

They both focused on their plates and the people walking by. They made no eye contact, and there was no further discussion other than Luisa telling Emille that Degas expected them for a lesson at the Louvre. They went back to the apartment to get their painting equipment. Emille added that they should not dwell on their conversation.

Taking In the Sun-Drenched Air
from the Fields of Crops

When Jean got up that morning, he found a letter from Monet. His humor didn't sound funny, which didn't surprise Jean. Monet said that if Jean hadn't sold his tree painting by then, he should give it away and come to Giverny to do his work as a gardener. Jean knew he should and would go to Giverny, probably that day. He already planned to meet Emille at the Louvre so she could contact Mr. and Mrs. Berléal about their portrait. At the moment, he thought he'd start in two weeks, and the work would take about two days. He felt sure Monet would approve of his coming back to paint their portrait, even if Monet seldom painted portraits himself. The only portrait Jean could remember by Monet was the one of his first wife as she died.

When he got to the Louvre after getting some breakfast at a café, he found Emille and Luisa painting while Degas walked back and forth between them, making comments to each and sometimes both.

"Jean, what are you doing here? You're interrupting the lessons," Degas said.

"Relax, Edgar. I'll only be a moment." He went to Emille and told her to contact the Berléals to tell them he would do the portrait over the course of two days in about two weeks. "Okay?" He nodded to Degas. "Sorry for the interruption, but my art business is important too."

Emille smiled and nodded. Luisa also smiled. Degas just looked hard, almost glaring at Jean as he left. Jean felt good about telling Degas that his art business was important. It wasn't teaching, but painting for pay was rewarding to Jean.

He had already packed his bag and brought it with him, so he went to the Saint-Lazare station, bought a ticket, and boarded the train when it got ready to depart. He got a window seat, put his bag next to him, took out his sketchbook, and reflected on the painting life. He tried to think about how he would pose the couple. Should he have one stand? When he got back to Paris, he promised himself he'd review the portraits of couples in the Louvre, something he knew he should have done, just like looking at what Monet had had him study.

He felt sleepy, so he opened the window, taking in the sun-drenched air from the fields of crops. The wind direction went across the train, so he didn't get smoke or steam from the engine. The fresh air felt good but didn't help him stay awake.

He woke when the train arrived at the station in Vernon. He got on the shuttle, on which he rode facing forward, and arrived at Giverny. He would try to find Monet after he got his room at the apartment house.

The intimate table for two in the entryway had a third chair. He smiled at the memory. Someday he hoped to sit there with just two chairs with Emille. The chance of that happening didn't overwhelm him, but he enjoyed the thought. He went inside; registered, getting his same room; put his bag down; and lay on the bed. Finally, his conscience got the best of him, and he got up to find Monet or the gardeners. When he went out, he put the third chair away.

Then Look and Then Stroke

Jean first went to the shed they used for the gardens, but he found no one who knew where the gardeners were working. He swung by Monet's studio and looked inside to see if Monet had taken his easels. He had. Jean went over the property in his mind. He'd been gone for just a few days, and he figured Monet would start at the point where they'd opened the water to make the pond. He could see that the days of digging had made sure the pond held a good level of water. He could also imagine Monet painting the pond before the plants went in. There looked to be a path along the pond, so he started to walk.

He found Monet at the narrow point where he planned to put a bridge—a Japanese bridge, he remembered. The first thing Monet said to him was "Where are the two ladies? Did you have any luck with either one?"

"Not that kind of luck, Claude. Emille did have a proposition for me."

"That's the one I figured you'd score with." Monet looked at the pond, dabbed his brush on his palette, and stroked the painting once.

"No, not that. She met a couple walking along the street with a Papillon. She talked to them and suggested they get their portrait painted. By me. And I don't have to share the money with her. She gets to paint the Papillon—named Coco, of course."

"When are you going to paint that? Aren't you working here in my gardens? Oh yes, you are an artist. When do you leave for Paris? Today?" Monet continued to paint a stroke at a time, focused more on the painting than on their conversation.

Jean went over to Monet's canvas and did some mental measurements and perspectives. "Claude, if I had scheduled painting the couple soon, I wouldn't have come here today. I told them two days of sitting for me in about two weeks. By the way, do you have any advice for me when I paint their portrait?"

"Is that why you came here?" Monet went back to work on his painting. "This is my before, since, if you remember, I'm going to put a bridge here."

"Japanese bridge, if I recall." Jean laughed because he'd said it before Monet could. Monet didn't laugh or say anything; he just resumed painting. Jean watched him. He always found it a pleasure to watch him paint. First, he'd look at his object, and then he'd make one or two quick strokes. He'd look and then stroke, almost as if the painting had become his dance partner. The painting quickly came to life as he worked. Jean still found it amazing how quickly Monet's paintings came alive.

"Jean, I like you. I see you are becoming a real artist. But portraits are painted inside. Do you think you can get them outside?" Monet usually found a way to push for his side of the inside versus outside argument.

"It depends on their place. I have been considering having them outside because of the papillon. Now I'll go find the gardeners, and we can talk more later. I do like the thought of painting the portrait outside, perhaps in their garden."

Luisa and Emille met Degas at a sidewalk café halfway up Montmartre and spent almost an hour in intense conversation while having only one glass of wine. At first, the fuss over the nude model and Degas's wanting them to pose in the same manner stood in the way of any reconciliation. Then Degas said, "Do you think

Mary Cassatt has posed nude? For me? For anyone? Of course not." Neither lady doubted what he said about Cassatt.

Silence enveloped the ladies as they continued to reflect on what Degas had set forth as a reason to compromise. Emille spoke first. "Then why can't we have the same arrangement with you? We're just like her. We have the same Philadelphia values. Both of us want to be artists. You have helped us improve our painting skills. Just drop the nude stuff."

Luisa looked up at the windows near the top of the building across the street. She couldn't tell if the windows had curtains.

"Luisa, do you feel the same way as Emille says she does?" Degas also looked up at the windows. She did not answer him. "I'll tell you what. I will not include nudes in the lessons I give you, with one exception."

"No exceptions, Mr. Degas." Luisa looked him directly in the eye. "None." Again, she looked up at the windows of the building.

"What if I had you paint the *Venus de Milo* statue? It's at the Louvre, and I'm sure you both have studied it. That's what artists do." Degas stood up.

Emille stood up as well, motioning for Luisa to remain seated. "I suspect we can deal with statues, though I only speak for myself. When I look at Luisa, who's sitting because I asked her to remain seated, I can't tell if Venus offends her. It offended her father, whom you met, I understand."

Luisa stood up and looked at Emille and then at Degas. "No nude models. None. If a piece of art with someone naked is in the Louvre and you take us to it, that is fine. We'll paint it if you ask us to do so. Is that a fair compromise? You say nudes help artists understand how persons are put together. The artwork at the Louvre will do the same for me, even if the artists got it wrong."

"Fine." Degas sat down. "I agree with your proposition and your requirements." He saw a waitress and waved to her. "Meet me at the Louvre tomorrow at the same time as before. By the way, Emille, how much of the day do you think about painting?"

"Quite a bit, I think. Especially if I am outside. There isn't much to see at our apartment."

"Except me," Luisa added.

"Emille, do you see shapes or colors?" Degas sounded like he did at their lessons.

"It depends. If it is a person, I see a shape, and if it is scene, like outdoors, I see color. Is that wrong?"

Degas didn't answer her. He asked the waitress for the bill.

"If it's a person," Luisa said, "she sees a man." She and Degas laughed.

"I think we have resolved our issues, and my questions are best saved for the lessons, ladies. I will pay the bill and see you tomorrow."

They both thanked him and began walking down the road. As soon as they were out of earshot, Emille asked Luisa what she had seen when she looked up.

"Emille, I looked at the windows at the top of the building across the street. I don't know why. Degas gave me so much pain."

"Perhaps you avoided him until he compromised. It's a fair arrangement for us."

Luisa took the lead down Montmartre, even swishing her skirt. Emille stayed close to her but tried not to draw attention to herself. Just before they reached the bottom of Montmartre, Luisa pointed to a café and offered to buy a bottle of wine.

And I Do Mean If

B ack in Giverny, Jean walked over almost the whole property and did not find the gardeners. He debated going to his apartment to get his things out of storage or going to find Monet again, who'd surely laugh at him for not asking where the gardeners were. Monet won, and Jean found him sitting on a green bench near his front door. A pretty young lady sat on the bench with him. She had some dirt on her skirt—probably, Jean thought, from doing some gardening. At least Monet had found something to distract him from painting. Jean wondered where Alice was while Monet spent time with his new friend.

"Jean!" Monet called out when he saw him approaching. "Meet my stepdaughter. She is Alice's daughter. Her name is Blanche. Blanche, this is Jean. He is an artist learning his craft. He is also a gardener and has worked here but not when you were here. Blanche spent a lot of time in Amsterdam, copying some of the greats of that city. She very much likes Van Gogh."

Jean walked up to them and nodded to Blanche, taking off his hat. She stood and offered him her hand. He accepted it, waited for her to sit back on the bench, and then sat on the bench across from her and her stepfather.

No one spoke after Jean sat down, until he broke the silence. "It is my pleasure to meet you, Blanche," he said to her. Then he looked at Monet. "Claude, do you enjoy sending people on pointless journeys? Where have you sent the gardeners?"

Monet laughed. "They have taken the large wagon to fill it with rocks. I want the entrance to the pond to have many rocks to keep the soil from washing downstream. And I let you go look for them because I wanted you to see what shape the pond is in. I'm hoping you'll have a suggestion or two."

Jean accepted what Monet had said and thought about what he might suggest.

"You treat him like you did us when we were growing up, Claude." Blanche didn't smile as she spoke. "Mr. Jean, it is my pleasure to meet you. I too am trying to be an artist. Perhaps there will be some time for us to compare notes." She stood up, waved to Monet, and went into the house.

Jean and Monet watched her walk away and go through the doorway. Jean thought she'd done the right thing in confronting Monet. He hoped it was a common interchange between the stepdaughter and her stepfather.

"If you talk with Blanche, and I do mean if, keep the topic on painting. I don't know when, but my hope is that she will marry my son, who is also named Jean. Most of all, tell your gardener friend Leon Duret to stay away from her. Anyone can see she is pretty, and I have seen how your friend reacts to her. She's spoken for. He won't do well if he doesn't stay away from her. And you know I mean what I'm saying."

Jean did know that Monet meant it, so he just sat on the bench, looking at his feet, saying nothing. Monet looked out at the path leading to the studio. He had his hand on his beard, posing as if thinking or maybe really thinking. Finally, he spoke. "Join us for dinner tonight, and I'll suggest a few topics for what you should paint while you are here." He stood and went into the house.

Jean sat for a bit and then went into the gardens, wondering if he would have the nerve to paint a portrait of Blanche. The more portraits he painted, the more his work would improve.

It Already Reached Late Afternoon

Jean felt relief when he saw the gardeners at the place where the stream entered the pond. They had a wagon full of rocks, some of which were as big as baskets for vegetables. He spoke with Leon, telling him that Monet would not tolerate anyone courting his stepdaughter. "Not you. Not me."

Leon went on and on about how beautiful she was and how her smile gave him hope. Then Monet showed up, and Jean told Leon to stay out of Monet's way.

Monet went over to the wagon filled with rocks. "These will do," he said loudly enough to be heard over the sound of water splashing on water. "See how the soil is moving downstream? Soon all your work will be washed away." He motioned for each gardener to look where the water poured into the pond.

When Leon's turn came, Monet glared at him. Jean wanted to remind Monet that Leon had been in charge of the gardeners when he went to sell his painting in Paris, but he kept quiet. He would do that at dinner.

"Put the rocks right in the hole," Monet said.

"Mr. Monet," one of the gardeners said, "do we get in the pond to place the rocks?"

"No. Roll the rocks one at a time quickly. Get a rhythm when you roll the rocks." He walked back, not wanting to have water splashed on him. He motioned to Jean that he should stay to talk with him rather than helping the gardeners. "I see you've spoken to Leon. I want him to stay away from Blanche, not away from me."

"That glare you gave Leon told him a lot. He needs the work. He'll do what you want about Alice's daughter. To change the subject, the rocks are a great idea."

The gardeners went to work, some taking the rocks out of the wagon and others rolling the rocks into the place in the pond where the stream entered. Soon they had the task completed.

"Good. Very good," Monet said. "Put the wagon back, and take the rest of the day off." Since it was already late afternoon, his suggestion didn't give the gardeners much of a reward.

Leon went to the other side of the wagon to avoid being seen by Monet. Jean felt sorry for him. He had a much better status with Monet than Leon did, but Jean also had no hope of finding a relationship with Monet's stepdaughter. He knew how Leon felt about Blanche. Then he realized he felt almost the same about Emille. He wiped his brow and gazed out at the pond. He saw the tree he had saved when he'd looked at the pond as a painting. He felt the weight of his memories of the gardens and enjoyed them.

"Jean, are you all right? You look stunned," Monet said. "Rolling the rocks shouldn't be seen as that big a deal. What's wrong?"

"Nothing, Claude. I guess I'm just amazed at how this project is coming along." He couldn't remember the first lie he'd told him years ago.

"Well, get yourself together. You do remember you are having dinner with me tonight, right? With us. And remember to talk only about art with Blanche."

"Claude, I'll be a proper guest this evening. I'm going to my apartment to clean up. Then I'll be at your place. Thanks for inviting me."

"Actually, Jean, I'm using you so I can practice keeping men away from Blanche."

"Does that mean that your Jean is not a man?"

Both of them laughed. Monet's smile went away quickly when Jean reminded him of how she'd gone into the house because of how Monet had treated him.

As He Made Eye Contact

Jean arrived at the front door of Monet's house and found Alice sitting on the green bench outside. He greeted her, and she suggested he sit on the bench facing her. They looked at each other for a while. Finally, she spoke. "Jean, Claude is trying to control my daughter Blanche. I understand you met her earlier today."

"That's right. I met her. Here in fact, on these benches. She is a lovely lady."

"I expected you would notice. Jean, I'm sitting here because I wanted to tell you that I don't disapprove of your interest in Blanche. You're nice, but you also live in Paris, which might be good for Blanche's interest in being an artist. She can't take lessons from Claude."

"Wait a minute, Alice. I said she is a lovely lady. That's all. I hope to enjoy talking about art with her. Not romance."

"I see. What about that gardener friend of yours? Does he want to talk to Blanche about gardening? Claude is particularly upset about that guy."

"Mr. Duret is a fine gentleman who depends on Mr. Monet for the work here. He has a house he would lose if he didn't have the work. I have told him that Mr. Monet does not want him near Blanche, and he will stay away from her." Jean looked at Alice but saw no reaction to what he had said. "Is it time for dinner?"

Alice simply nodded and got up. He held the door for her and then waited a bit before going inside. Alice had already taken her place at the table, at Monet's side.

Another man sat quietly at the foot of the table, where Monet often told Jean to sit. He looked at Claude, not knowing where Monet would put him.

"Jean, do come in. There is another Jean at the foot of the table: my son Jean Monet. Shake his hand, and then sit here next to Alice."

Jean and Jean shook hands, and then he sat next to Monet's wife. Neither mentioned having talked about Blanche. Several minutes later, Blanche and her five siblings came in to take their places at the table. Claude made sure they all sat where he wanted them. Jean nodded to each of them as he made eye contact.

The first course, Camembert fritters with apple and raisin

chutney, grabbed Jean's attention because it was one of his favorite starter courses, as it was for many. Claude said nothing, and Blanche's siblings chatted about something they had been doing, but Jean didn't pay attention to them. Blanche and Jean Monet looked at each other frequently but didn't say anything. Nothing changed as they had the second course, pork, and then dessert.

Dinner quietly ended. The siblings rushed off, as did Alice. Claude and Jean, plus Blanche and Jean Monet, eased back in their chairs.

Jean decided he might as well say what he had been thinking. "Claude, remember that I told you I am going to do a portrait when I get back to Paris?"

Monet stood up. "Where are you going with this?"

"I thought Blanche and your son Jean could pose for me since the portrait in Paris will also be a couple. It's just a thought."

Claude looked at the couple and then at him. "Fine. The couple, Jean and Blanche, will sit for you tomorrow, and you can do your thing."

"Oh, thank you. I'm hoping to do the portrait in Paris outside, perhaps in the couple's garden. It will be a step forward for me." Jean could not think of anything else to say to have Monet approve the portrait.

"I know the place," Monet said. "Tomorrow the four of us will meet outside here in the morning. I will give each of you some advice."

Blanche seemed to be ignoring what Jean Monet said to her, just as she clearly ignored Jean as well as her stepfather.

He Doesn't Have Any of His Own Gardens

Jean left Monet's house feeling good that he would get to paint the portrait he had hoped to do. He didn't feel good about Monet being there when he painted. He had his own ideas on what to do, based on what he had learned from John Singer Sargent when he met him in London. Sargent was famous for painting portraits. Monet didn't know about that trip, and neither did Degas. But Jean's self-portrait and the painting of the well-endowed woman were proof he knew what to do. He didn't want or need Monet's advice.

On his walk back to his apartment, he realized Monet seemed to be giving him more time to be an artist and demanding less of his time as a gardener. Maybe, he thought, Claude was doing so because while Jean loved gardening, he didn't have any of his own gardens. Monet probably had gardens at most of, if not all, the places he lived. Jean lived in Paris and had no wife or lover. Even if he had, how could he have afforded to buy a property with a garden? He liked to garden, but had to admit he'd learned the skill there in Giverny to make money and to learn about Monet's art.

Jean stopped and rubbed his hair with both hands. Monet was one of the best artists alive and maybe of all time. Why shouldn't Jean want that artist to teach him something? He was doing Jean Monet and Blanche's portrait for practice, not for money. Monet wouldn't be with him in Paris when he did get paid for a portrait. He felt better about having Monet at the portrait session tomorrow.

Jean also decided to avoid his friend Leon that evening, so he wouldn't have to tell him everything he'd seen Blanche do at dinner. He had a bottle of Bordeaux wine in his room. Drinking it at the little table would be a nice way to end the day, he decided. He could think about Emille as well.

When he arrived at the apartment, the third chair had been brought out again. No one sat at the table, but there was a bit of a mess, so he could tell three people had been there earlier. He got his wine along with an opener, a glass, and a rag to clean up the table. He also put the third chair away. He thought of Blanche and Jean Monet. How would he pose them? *The couple in Paris are married and will have the Papillon on at least one of their laps.* He planned to have them both sitting in a nice place rather than standing—but not too nice a setting, because portraits were about the people.

Tomorrow, he knew, Blanche wouldn't want Jean Monet to be too close or too intimate. But Monet might. Jean opened the wine, sat back, and toasted his being an artist. He also remembered the times when Emille and Luisa had sat at that table with him. Someday, he thought as he poured a second glass, he and Emille would sit there. He toasted to that as well.

He Is Holding Her Two Fingers

The next morning, Jean waited a while after breakfast, and then brought his easel and canvas to the front of Monet's house. Blanche and Jean were sitting on one of the green benches, and Claude paced back and forth aggressively. He waved for Jean to hurry when Blanche pointed to his arrival. "Let's go. I have decided that the portrait will be along the pond. I have a bench for them there." He waved at Blanche and his son almost as if he tried to pull them by their ears.

Jean thought for a moment and then decided it didn't matter where they sat. He didn't want to argue with Monet. Anyway, the couple in Paris would sit, or stand, where he decided.

"Here," Monet said as they approached the bench. "Son, you sit here, and, Blanche, you sit next to him. Put your arm around her."

"No, Claude, Jean and I are not like that with each other," Blanche said.

The two of them did sit on the bench, and Jean quickly started to sketch them.

Jean had another idea, but he didn't want to start an argument. Everyone remained silent, and then Jean said, "Claude, remember the painting at the Louvre titled *Portrait of a Couple*, painted in 1610 by an unknown master? The man is gently holding the woman's left hand by the two fingers above her ring finger. He is clean shaven and wearing a wide-brimmed black hat, a white collar that extends from his neck to his shoulders over a large cloak, and calf-length pants. His white socks and black shoes contrast nicely.

She has a similar white collar with a locket on a chain. Her dress is dark in color, dark brown and almost black."

"Who cares about what they're wearing? Paint these two as they are dressed."

"I only mentioned the clothing so you would remember the painting. My point is that he is holding her two fingers."

"I remember the painting. They are standing up. Paint these two sitting, and if you want him to hold Blanche's two fingers, that's fine. The couple in Paris are married to each other, not related, as these two are."

"We're not related, Claude, and we certainly aren't married to each other," Blanche said, and Jean Monet nodded vigorously.

Monet looked up at the sun and then walked off, saying he had a painting to work on. His son followed him. Blanche stayed on the bench until they were out of sight. "Sorry this didn't work out," she said, "but I did learn something about portraits."

"I suspect I could learn from you, Blanche. Painting is all Claude is allowing me to talk about with you. Which is fine."

"Do you have a girlfriend? If not, I hope you find one. You are good looking enough. Good luck." She said nothing more but smiled at Jean and then left, walking in the direction Claude had gone.

Jean took his easel and canvas to a bench in the garden to finish the sketch. Jean's memory of the attempted portrait wasn't all that good. He struggled to get an expression of affection on Blanche's face. Monet's son looked okay, but the look was not exactly what Jean hoped to achieve. *But it's a sketch*, he told himself.

He Told Monet What the Note Said

Blanche, who came back about an hour after the group disbanded. He heard her walking through the tall grass and then watched her stride toward him. He smiled.

"Jean, I'm glad I found you. Claude told me to get you to come to him. Apparently, someone sent a letter to you at his address. Oh, let me see what you have done." She reached for the sketchbook.

"It's a sketch, Blanche. I'm glad you are here. Pose for me for just a few minutes, and then I'll go to Claude."

She gave him the sketchbook and then sat back in her place and looked at Jean, as she had earlier. He saw what he had done wrong and adjusted the angle of her face more toward Monet's son in the sketch. He expected that Monet would like her showing interest in his son.

On the walk back to Monet's house, Blanche told him about seeing a large collection of paintings by Vincent Van Gogh. She essentially bragged about seeing *The Starry Night*, a painting he had heard of but not seen. She praised a painting titled *Crows over a Wheat Field*, describing it in detail because he mentioned that he had not heard of that one. They had just started talking about Van Gogh's death, when they caught up with Monet.

"Jean, come here. What were you two talking about?"

"Vincent Van Gogh," Blanche replied, and then she left them.

"Well, that's good. Blanche likes his paintings. Anyway, here is a letter addressed to you that was sent to my address. I haven't opened it." He almost tossed it to him. "Some of Alice's friends have sent her letters addressed to 'Alice and Claude Monet,' essentially putting her in charge of the family. She's not in charge. Alice is a traditional French lady who understands her role. You need to understand your role here. As does the woman who wrote this."

Jean took the letter and noted that there was no return address. Inside was a short note from Emille, telling him that Charles Berléal and his wife had scheduled a trip to America in two weeks and would be gone for two months. She also wrote that she'd said she would have Jean call on them the day after tomorrow. He told Monet what the note said and then showed it to him to make it clear that was all Emille had said, other than a bit about meeting him at the Louvre tomorrow.

"This is from the lady who propositioned you, Jean? She has good handwriting."

Monet had to joke to get rid of his anger. While Jean had known Claude for years, he still didn't know why he had his fits. Did getting a letter addressed to someone else at his home upset him that much? Or at all? Monet's first question had been about what Jean and Blanche had talked about. He closed his eyes and shrugged. That had to be the reason.

"Let me see what you've done in your sketch pad." Monet took it from Jean and held it so the sunlight shone on the sketch. "My son looks bored. Have him sit up straighter. Blanche looks good. I like how you have her face at an angle to show her interest in him. I'd appreciate it if you would actually make a portrait of them and give it to me."

Jean said he would do as he asked, and they chatted a bit. Then each of them went back to what he wanted to do. Jean decided to work on the sketch at the table for two outside his apartment building. He would also pack and catch a late train to Paris.

Does God Answer Your Prayers?

On Sunday, Monet gave in and took Alice to Rouen—in a taxi rather than driving his motorcycle, which she would not ride on. He went into his studio across from the cathedral to work on one of the paintings of that structure. The sunlight was just right.

Alice went to Mass in the cathedral, received communion, and spoke to the priest as she left worship. After she told him her name and relationship to Monet, he said he would talk with her in the park. She followed some women the priest said were going there. She found an empty bench, sat down, and relaxed. She saw Monet open the back door to the studio. He waved to her and then shut the door while staying inside. She also saw the priest, who talked briefly with several parishioners at different benches. He came up to Alice, pointed to her bench, and said, "May I sit here? My name is Monsignor Jacques Hamel."

"Yes, Monsignor, it would be helpful for me to talk with you."

"Do you need to go to confession? This is private enough." He bowed his head as if to pray.

"I do need your prayers, but I have been to confession about all that Claude and I did that was sinful. What I pray for every day is that my husband, Claude Monet, will spend more time with me. I only see him at meals. We even have separate bedrooms. He is either off somewhere painting, like now up in that studio, or he is gardening. Oh, I try to watch him paint, but he gets agitated if I say a word. If I watch him garden, he puts me to work."

Monsignor Hamel bowed his head, made the sign of the cross, and then prayed for her as she had asked. He ended the prayer, saying, "Amen," and sat up straight. "I will pray for you every day. How long will your husband be painting here in Rouen?"

Alice looked up at the studio while wiping her eyes with her hands. "He's almost finished with this one, but I'm sure he plans to paint more versions of the cathedral. It's beautiful, by the way. The problem is that the next one will be at a different time of day. A different angle of the sun." The door to the studio opened while she still had her eyes on it. Monet waved to her, indicating she should come up. She waved back, pointing to Monsignor Hamel and waving that Monet should come down to her. She prayed to herself that he would do as she asked.

"Do you think he will come down here? I have other parishioners to talk with."

"Monsignor, please. Let's see if he does quickly." Almost as she spoke, they saw Monet appear on one side of the studio and start his way down to them.

"Oh Lord, make this a nice visit," Alice said.

Monsignor Hamel prayed aloud so she could hear him, focusing on God making each of them understand the other. He stood up as Monet reached the bench, holding out his hand. Claude shook his hand and then patted Alice on her shoulder.

"Good morning, Monsignor, and thank you for speaking with my wife, Alice. She has been anxious to meet with you. And as I understood you to say when I first met you, yes, you should visit my gardens. Is there an afternoon and evening when you could come to dinner?"

They agreed on a date a week and two days from then. Monsignor Hamel then excused himself, saying that other parishioners were waiting for him. He blessed Claude and Alice and then left them. Monet seemed to Alice to have stood tall for the blessing.

While You Finish Your Glass of Wine

Jean had no trouble getting back to Paris. He went to his studio to drop off the sketch of Monet's son and Blanche. He thought he had it the way he wanted it and the way it should be. Monet had rightly noted the angle of Blanche's face, which Jean had drawn to please Monet. She had looked at him when he started the sketch, for whatever reason.

He went to the Café de la Nouvelle Athénes for lack of anything better to do. It felt early enough to have a bit of red wine and not late enough to go to sleep. He joined the group, briefly saying he had been at Giverny for a few days. Then he listened to the talk.

Pissarro told of making plans for a showing. "We impressionists need a good event to make some serious money. Degas is going to have some of his ballet dancer paintings." He went around the tables, inviting others to tell what they could bring. As a group, Jean thought they were lucky to have Paul Cézanne and Camille Pissarro with them, which didn't always happen. The attendance by authors and other intellectuals also helped the artists understand their world better. Émile Zola's contributions opened Jean's eyes on several topics, especially the recent talks about the miracles at the Lourdes ministry site. He avoided looking at Cézanne when Zola talked about that topic. Jean had calmed down about Zola while continuing to reflect on his faith. Or lack of faith.

When he poured a glass of wine for himself, he saw Luisa and Camille at a table farther inside the café. He hadn't noticed them when he came in, because he had focused on the gathered artists. After he told the artists to save his seat, he took his glass with him as he went over to them. "Good evening, ladies. It is nice to see you again."

Luisa stood up and offered her hand for him to shake. "Mr.

Jean, we are relaxing after a long day. Degas had Emille and me at his studio for many hours today, and Camille has just finished her shift as a waitress. How did Giverny go? And Monet? Sit with us while you finish your glass of wine."

He sat down across from the two ladies. "Giverny stays the same always. But I did meet Monet's son, also named Jean, and his stepdaughter Blanche. Claude seems to think they will make a nice couple. I started a portrait of the two of them." He didn't mention the portrait Emille had arranged for him.

"I'm sure it will be wonderful, like your portrait I bought of that lady. Do you remember her name?"

"No, Luisa, she's gone from my life," he said almost as if he had anticipated her question. It hadn't been easy, but he had forgotten not only her name but also her as a person.

Camille spoke for the first time. "I hope you will bring that portrait to Paris so I can see it. I like portraits."

"Don't say it, Jean," Luisa said quickly.

"Say what?" Camille asked. She looked at Luisa and then at him. "Does she mean a portrait of the two of us? Or Luisa and Emille?"

"I didn't have either of those portraits in mind, ladies." He finished his glass of wine, stood up, tipped his hat, and then motioned to the artists. "I am going back with them. Enjoy your rest."

They Sat in the Shade

Jean stayed with the artists until he finished his bottle of wine; then he went home to bed. The conversation had focused on painting the sky, which he appreciated. Jean had not thought much about skies so far in his artwork. His two paintings of trees included the sky, but he hadn't really explored what he could do with it. That surprised him because Monet did such a wonderful rendition of the sky. The Rouen cathedral paintings showed it even more than the hay bale paintings because of the sky's effect on the building.

The next morning, he went about his usual routine, finishing with breakfast at a small café near his studio. He then walked slowly in the Louvre, taking his time to look at the wonderful art. Eventually, he found his way to the gallery where Degas had Emille and Luisa copying the same Rembrandt painting as before. He didn't interrupt them but sat nearby, close enough so he could see what each lady did with her paintbrush. He alternated his attention, comparing how each lady treated each feature in the Rembrandt.

Finally, Degas stood, telling the ladies they were done for the day. "I know we usually work longer, but I have something to do this afternoon. Emille, you won't be with me tomorrow. Luisa, come to my studio tomorrow. I'll have a surprise for you. It will be a nice surprise."

While the ladies packed up their art supplies, Jean shook his hand when Degas came over to him. "I liked what I saw with the ladies' painting. Different but very nice."

"Jean, saying 'Very nice' tells me you favor one over the other."

"Not if favoring means liking the paintings," Luisa said, walking past with her equipment. "And don't worry, Mr. Degas; I won't let the paint smear. See you at your studio tomorrow. Remember your promise."

Degas laughed, not telling Jean what his promise had been.

Emille walked by right behind Luisa. "Jean, I want to talk to you about the Berléal mansion. Some of the rooms are so beautiful." She looked to be bursting with excitement.

"Tell me about it at lunch. Maybe I'll see you tonight, Edgar. Have a good afternoon." He didn't help Emille carry her equipment. He was a gentleman and would have helped, but she wanted to be an artist. Being responsible for one's equipment was part of it.

They left the Louvre and walked a short way to a café for lunch. They sat in the shade. As soon as they sat at their table, Emille started telling him about the house where Coco lived. She described the beautiful herringbone parquet flooring, moldings, and many fireplaces, almost breathless in her excitement. "The ground floor has an entrance hall, a double living and reception room with an ornate fireplace, a dining room, and a fitted kitchen. Three bedrooms, a study, a bathroom, a shower room, and a toilet are upstairs. The top floor comprises a master suite with a bathroom, a toilet with two dressing rooms, and a guest bedroom. The basement includes a laundry room and a wine cellar."

"Emille, you sound so excited about this house. I can visualize it just from your detailed description—your verbal painting. Maybe you should be a professional architect instead of an artist. Just kidding. Where does Coco go outside?"

She breathed heavily, rocking back and forth with her eyes closed. "The front door has an area with couches and chairs. It is surrounded by big bushes on three sides, with the house itself on the fourth side. Coco has a little fenced-in area. Why?"

"I'm thinking of painting the portrait outside. Monet suggested it. I like the idea because Coco is their dream dog. Dogs belong outside. But we'll see when we talk to them in the morning. It will be up to them."

Because of the Dog

Later that evening, when Jean went to Café de la Nouvelle Athénes, Emille and Luisa were there, with Luisa facing the bar where Camille filled the drink orders. Camille saw him and picked up a bottle of pinot noir. He nodded and sat near Emille, who sat next to Luisa. Degas had not come that evening.

Jean noticed that both ladies had a glass of wine. When Camille's shift as waitress ended, she came to the table. Emille got up, moved to an empty chair across from Jean, and presented her glass for some of his wine. Camille had a bottle of wine and sat in the chair Emille had left. Jean saw Emille's move as accepting Luisa's interest in Camille, not as reflecting Emille's interest in him. *Unfortunately*, he thought. However, she could have moved farther away from him. Was it just his wine that she wanted? Then he smiled at her anyway.

Renoir began to recall a conversation he'd had with Camille Pissarro and Jean-Baptiste-Camille Corot long ago that addressed the indoors versus outdoors debate some of them were having. He told Luisa and Emille to sit still and not disturb his story, which, to Jean, meant Renoir had not accepted them yet. "Jean, you will like this. Pissarro said that an artist is to work at the same time upon sky, water, branches, and ground, so you are keeping everything going on an equal basis. You are to rework without stopping until you have what you are trying to paint. This conversation took place so many years ago, and I can still hear him say, 'It is best not to lose the first impression,' and he painted unhesitatingly."

Jean liked that and said so.

Renoir went on. "Now, Corot completed his scenic paintings back in his studio. He revised them back to his preconceptions. Pissarro painted what he saw, which is different. They asked me to comment, and I simply said that I don't compare art or artists; plus, I like both of their works. What do you think, Jean?"

Jean took a sip of wine before he replied. "Well, neither Monet nor Degas is here tonight to shout at each other. Earlier this week, I started a portrait of Monet's son Jean and his stepdaughter. Outside, of course. Tomorrow I am going to start a portrait of a couple and their papillon. I plan to pose them outdoors because of the dog. I understand the couple has some very nice furniture inside." He nodded to Emille. "But I think that outside will focus directly on the couple."

Several of the artists at the table murmured in agreement. Pissarro shook his head. "Jean, if that were true, more of the portraits at the Louvre, for example, would have the people outside. But they are in delightful rooms, with many objects to testify about who they are. I understand these two ladies have been working on a Rembrandt portrait of the holy family indoors, though there is light shining in."

"I saw both of their work," Jean said. "But remember, Van Gogh had some portraits of himself, but you can't tell if he is inside or not. They focus on himself. That's what I want to do. Besides, the couple is wealthy, so their clothes, along with maybe part of the mansion as background, will show that they are important. You do agree that having wealth is important, right? Or being wealthy?"

After both yes and no opinions were offered, they chatted a while longer. Jean told Emille to meet him for breakfast at the café where they'd had lunch earlier that day. Then he left to go home, wondering what Emille would do before going to her apartment.

You Are a Virgin

Not long after he left the café, Jean heard rapid footsteps behind him—clearly a lady running, because they were light, not pounding like a man's. He turned to see Emille come up to him. She pressed herself into him. "Jean!" she screamed. "Luisa is taking Camille to her room in our apartment. What can I do?"

He patted her shoulder and ran his hand along the back of her neck. "Calm down. Tell me what has you upset Are you jealous?"

She stayed close, not puffing as much. "Not in a million years. Why would I even think of jealousy?" She sighed. "Thanks. Luisa and I talked about this a day or so ago. I said I wouldn't care if she and Camille were in her bedroom."

"What did she say?"

"I don't want to tell you."

"Why not?" He put his hands on her shoulders, not pushing but holding her steady, while he eased back to separate them. He'd been wanting a hug from her or Luisa for a long time but not that way. While he waited for her to speak, he thought about the hug. He still had hope but not at that moment.

Emille stepped back and looked at him with a frown. "Luisa said she wouldn't care if I had you in my bedroom." She covered her face with her hands, starting to cry, almost groaning with her sobs.

"Is that what you want tonight?" He quickly regretted saying it, but maybe it hadn't been wrong to ask her what she wanted. He couldn't figure it out yet.

"No. Well, no." She walked around almost as if she danced a waltz without having a partner. "No."

Jean thought Emille showed she could dance nicely. "What you and I do, Emille, if we ever do anything—and I'm not suggesting that we do anything tonight or ever—should have nothing to do with what Luisa does. I need to tell you I'm not upset with Luisa and Camille. It isn't my business. I care for you.

The silence now seemed "I care a lot for you, but caring alone will not lead to anything happening between us. Caring for each other is not enough to make something happen."

"Jean, if we, say, were in my bedroom, would we, you know, do it?" She waltzed around again, and he wanted to be her partner.

"You are a virgin. You are saving yourself for the man you will spend your life with. It won't be me unless you and I are sure it is me. Then we will get physical. But not now. Let me walk you home, but I won't come in. By the way, when I relaxed at Giverny, I sat at the table for two. After I put the third chair away, I wished you were there."

"Jean, sitting at a table is a lot more likely than what we've just said. Yes, you can walk me home, and I trust you to do as you promised."

He walked up to her, held her in a dance frame, waltzed a bit, and then released her. He took her hand and started to walk. She stood tall, as if she continued to dance. Her strides had a rhythm he liked.

We Still Can Be Painting Partners

Emille went up to her apartment after saying good night to Jean. He kept his promise and didn't come in with her. He just walked away, not looking back to see if she had turned to watch him. When she got upstairs to her apartment, she found Luisa sitting on the couch alone.

"Good evening, Emille. Before you sit down, please look in my bedroom to confirm that Camille is not here. She didn't come here, but I want you to be sure about that. And it is no surprise that I wanted to know if you brought Jean here."

After looking in Luisa's bedroom, Emille looked also in her own bedroom. "Jean did walk me home, but we didn't even kiss. When I left you, I raced after him from the café, and when I caught up with him, I hugged him. I cried. I told him I didn't approve of you bringing Camille here. He wanted to know why that bothered me. I stopped crying then because I didn't know why I cried. Oh, then it occurred to me that our culture considers that to be immoral. I'm not French, and neither are you. I should have understood that." Emille put her hands on her hips. "We then talked about our possible relationship. He told me I need to wait for the man I will spend the rest of my life with, and when or if we are sure it is him, we can get together that way. He is so proper. He even said that I am a virgin. I am, of course."

"I believe you, and also, I understand now. Camille declined to come here because—well, she had her reasons. I don't think she is a virgin. Oh, when she declined, I hadn't asked her to come with me. It seemed sort of like an open question. I don't know what I would have done."

"You don't even know if she's been married." Emille slumped in the stuffed chair across from the couch, where Luisa sat. "And neither of us knows if Jean is or has been married. Oh, I'm so confused."

Luisa held up her sketchbook. "See what I did. I kind of like this sketch of you and Jean. I'm not going to finish the one I started of Camille and me. I tore it up while I waited for you to come home tonight." She put the sketchbook down. "When we have talked, you and I have used the term *Boston marriage*. That's why we have two bedrooms but one apartment. Why don't we continue this arrangement? What we do will only be our business. Some people say that men consider Boston marriages to be useful in helping women be prepared for marriage to a man. I want to be an artist. I think you do too. We are painting partners."

"I know." Emille buried her head in her arms. "I do want to be an artist—even more. Plus, we still can be painting partners. I'm going with Jean tomorrow to watch and learn as he paints the portrait. I'm going to paint Coco too. But this will be totally a painting event, like your lesson with Degas tomorrow."

The ladies stood and hugged each other, and each went to her own bedroom.

He Tried to Have a Vision

When Jean left Emille at her apartment, he decided to go back to the café for a bit more wine. He had shown calmness for her sake, but *calm* didn't describe how he felt now. He smiled when he thought that if he were Emille, he would have been waltzing with himself. He would be happy to sit with some wine—alone, he hoped. Most of the artists should have left the café.

When he walked into the café, he frowned when he saw Camille still at their table, now alone. She saw him and waved him over. "Sit down, Jean. I have some wine and can't persuade myself to drink it. Here's a clean glass too." After handing him the glass, she rested her face on her hands with her elbows on the table.

He sat, poured the wine, and smiled. "You must like being here, as it's after work and all. Thanks for the wine. I need some to relax or calm down."

"Why? What happened?"

He lied to her. "I have spent a lot of time thinking about the portrait I'm going to paint, or start anyway. Tomorrow." Because Camille was sitting there in the café with him, he knew she wasn't in bed with Luisa. She didn't need to know about Emille. "Did Luisa and Emille leave together?"

"No, Emille left in a big hurry. Luisa said something to her that I didn't hear. She almost ran out the door. Luisa finished her wine and left, going slowly. More like normally, I should say. The two of them seem to be under a lot of stress. Have you noticed?" Camille's smile became even more engaging. "Degas has asked me to model for him. I feel good about that. I think it is a compliment. You are a good painter too. I loved the self-portrait you had here. If I remember, Emille bought it." She looked intently at him and then relaxed. She sat up straighter in her chair. "Are you looking at me to see if I would be a good model for you? Would you hire me? I have a good figure."

"Camille, you are a lovely woman."

"Do you paint nudes? Degas does, and that's what he's going to do with me. He showed me two of his nudes. Of ballet dancers."

Jean sat in silence, poured more wine he didn't need, and adjusted his tie. He stalled as much as he could. Finally, he shrugged. "Camille, I don't know what to say. I do know that when I paint, I try to have a vision of what I'm trying to do with the subject. I am sitting here trying to figure out what my vision of you in the nude would possibly be." He thought but didn't say that he had no interest in painting nudes and certainly not her.

"Is it about your vision of me? Or is it about what else you would do with me? You can tell me the truth. I understand painters. At least some of them." She stretched in a way that seemed to invite an embrace.

"Well, I believe that each artist is different from all the others, just like their paintings are different. I'm not like Degas, who does paint nudes, and I'm also not like Monet, who doesn't, to my knowledge, paint nudes. Anyway, thanks for the wine. I need to go home to get some rest for my portrait appointment tomorrow."

He started to get up, when she reached for his hand. "Don't leave yet. You haven't answered my question. About your vision of me."

He pulled his hand back, bowed to her, said nothing, and left. He went home.

A Plumb Line in His Left Hand

In the morning, he had breakfast with Emille before they headed to the home of Charles and Suzanne Berléal for the portrait work. He didn't tell her about seeing Camille and finding out about her posing nude for Degas. Emille didn't say anything about what, if anything, had happened when she got to her apartment. She only said that Luisa would be going to Degas's studio for a lesson. Both Jean and Emille wanted to focus on the portrait.

After breakfast, he had a taxi take them to the house. When they arrived, he immediately saw why Emille had been so impressed by the structure. Coco came out to greet Emille and then pranced around both Emille and Jean. Charles Berléal wore a nice black suit with a black tie and hat. Suzanne Berléal wore a white dress that had a brown ring at her neck, shoulders, wrists, waist, and hemline. Both looked formal as well as wealthy, as did the glorious house.

Jean walked up to them, offered his hand, and introduced himself. Mr. Berléal put his hand out for him to shake. "My name is Charles," he said. "Please call me that. Call my wife Suzanne. We will not be formal with you."

Jean mentioned that he thought the portrait should be outside, saying it would be more natural for Coco. He added that he'd had a papillon when growing up.

Charles said he expected him to paint their portrait inside the house. He led him on a tour of the main floor. Jean posed them different ways and then asked if he could at least pose them outside, on one of the delightful benches. Coco would be on Suzanne's lap, he added. When he found the right bench, he had Emille replace Charles so he could see the overall picture, including the house in the background.

Without saying anything to Suzanne, Charles agreed that pose at that place would be fine. Jean thought Charles felt the structure of the house outside showed their status better than any of the admittedly lovely rooms inside. Jean felt even surer that the outside setting would produce the most impressive portrait. He also saw Charles's agreement with his suggestion as a positive sign that Charles trusted him.

It took Jean about half an hour to get set up with the easel, paints, and palette. Then he had the couple return to their pose. Coco jumped right up onto Suzanne's lap. Jean drew them with his brush, starting with the outside of their heads and then sketching in the bodies. He held a plumb line in his left hand to ensure he stayed true to the vertical. He used charcoal to place the heads and shoulders to ensure the exact locations of the heads, necks, shoulders, and bodies. He located the eyes and other features of their faces, revising the expressions until he had what he saw. He felt proud to know them that well after the little time he had been with them.

"Charles, Suzanne, this is what I need for now. Let's take a break."

"Fine," Charles said, snapping his fingers to have a servant come out. "Please, you and Emille can join us for lunch." He escorted them inside with intense dignity. Suzanne fussed with Coco and brought the dog inside with them.

Lunch gave Jean even more of an understanding of the house and the couple. It also gave him his first taste of what Emille later told him was American-style cooking: steak and potatoes. The dessert was French: individual bowls of ice cream with chocolate sauce.

Charles slipped little treats to Coco, who reached out to his knee when he ignored him. Suzanne commented that she preferred for Coco to eat dog food, which had the needed nutrition for the pet, and then affirmed Charles's spoiling Coco. Emille also gave the pet a treat. Jean decided he would not do so.

If the Portrait Is Accurate

After lunch, Jean had the couple resume their pose. He let Coco romp with Emille since he thought it would be unfair to have Coco sit on Suzanne's lap for that long. He also wanted Emille to have time to at least sketch Coco.

When Charles and Suzanne seemed to be tiring even after several breaks, Jean finally felt he had everything he needed in the portrait to begin to put in color, shading, and details. He thought he could do that from memory. He asked Charles when they were leaving for America.

"In just over a week," Suzanne said. Charles looked at his watch.

Jean said, "I will take the canvas to my studio and work as long as necessary to finish it before you leave for America."

Charles stood up, shook his hand, and then called for and paid a taxi to take Jean to his studio. Emille would ride with him.

They both sat in the backseat of the taxi. Jean held the portrait on his knees, not thinking about blocking the rear view. The taxi driver asked him to lower the painting, so Jean moved his legs to the side so he could set the painting on the floor.

"What are those dabs of color on both of their faces?" Emille pointed to the canvas. "They look tan almost."

"Those dabs, as you call them, are what I decided the color of their skin would be. She has lighter skin than he does. I don't remember color as well as I do shape. And don't tell Monet that." He laughed.

"So that's why I saw you mixing colors on your palette. I wondered how you would remember enough to produce a complete portrait. Do you think Charles is wondering that too? What if he doesn't like it? What if Suzanne doesn't either?"

"It doesn't matter if he doesn't like it. Or if she doesn't. What I mean is that honest portraits show who people are. They may not like the fact that they are smiling not enough or too much, but if the portrait is accurate, it truly doesn't matter. Of course, if I painted something that wasn't accurate, it would clearly matter, and I'd have to change it. I'm sure they understand, based on the original art on their walls, and I hope they will like what I paint. I see this portrait as a wonderful challenge to create a work of art that is as nice as what they have in their house. Really, they look so good sitting there with Coco and with part of the house in the picture."

"Well, that's interesting, but I'm still wondering if he trusts you to remember what you haven't drawn yet."

"He hasn't paid me yet. Don't worry; I'll do just fine. I'm anxious to continue work on this. That's why I'm dropping you off at your apartment and then going to my studio to do more work on it today. And tomorrow. And day after day until it is done. Done the way I know I can do it."

They reached her apartment and shook hands. She got out of the taxi, waved, and went inside. The driver took Jean to his studio, where he began work on the portrait. He positioned the canvas to have almost the same light as it had at their home. Jean worked on getting the colors visible on his palette to use when the time came. He had now become a portrait painter, doing what he loved to do, and he did it well. Jean worked on the portrait until he had to get some sleep.

Don't You See the Intensity?

When Emille went into her apartment after Jean dropped her off there, she found Luisa sitting in her usual place on the couch. Luisa had a letter in her hand. "Emille, let's go for a walk." She stood up and went to the door.

"Why a walk? What's in that letter? I'm tired. I don't need to walk after helping Jean work on the portrait and playing with Coco." Emille leaned back on her chair.

"Please," Luisa said, going out the door.

Emille followed, bringing her sketchbook, hoping she would hear good news, though she expected it to be a problem. She thought Luisa was acting strangely and didn't appear to have been drinking.

Luisa led them to Montmartre, where they walked until she found a café with a table almost in the road. The café wasn't as far up the road as the café where they met with Degas. Emille thought that good had resulted from that meeting, so maybe this one would also be good.

"Sit down, Emille. This letter has some heavy news."

Emille looked up at her. "I'm sitting, so read it to me."

Luisa stood in front of Emille and read the letter, which her father had sent from his home in Bryn Mawr, Pennsylvania. "Dad wrote, 'I understand that you and your artist friend Emille are preparing to or even have already established what I have learned is called a Boston marriage. It is not at all a Philadelphia marriage and for damn sure is not a Bryn Mawr marriage. You are ordered by me, your father, the head of our family, to find your own place to stay to study art. I'm willing to let you stay in Paris, but you must do it properly. I don't believe you have been the young woman I raised you to be. I have spoken with Mary Cassatt's father, whose daughter has become a fine painter since she has lived the life of a dignified woman. He tells me she does not have a personal relationship with that Degas artist who has taught her so much. In truth, she does not have a personal relationship with anyone.' I can't read any more, Emille." Luisa sat at the table, waving away a waitress.

Emille waved the waitress back, ordered an absinthe, and then looked at Luisa, almost glaring at her painting partner, wondering if "painting partners" was still the right description of their relationship. "You are going to move out? Are you going to move in with Camille? I know you like her more than as a waitress in a café."

"Emille, stop talking about Camille. I only told you about her coming with me to my room—which was a lie, as you saw when you got home—to get you to be jealous. I really hoped to bring us together. It didn't. No, I'm not going to move in, as you call it, with Camille. I shouldn't tell you this, but Camille poses nude for Degas. She says it is just posing, but I don't think so. I don't trust either of them. And neither should you. But that's Paris. In fact, I leave tomorrow for Philadelphia. I'm going back to Bryn Mawr. For now. I will find a way to study painting."

"Wait. This is important in your life. And mine. I have my sketchbook. Let me sketch you reading the letter to me. Then you finish it by showing me sitting on my chair with you reading to me."

"Why? Who cares?" Luisa looked at the letter again. "Do you think it is likely most artists would paint a woman reading a letter to another woman?"

"Don't you see the intensity? Why would a woman read a letter to another woman? You read it to me because it affirmed something. In our case, it is you telling me that you are going to leave me and go back home. Why else does one woman read a letter to another? Aren't there good reasons?"

"Name one."

They didn't say anything more while the waitress brought Emille her absinthe, other than Luisa declining to have one herself. Luisa got up, said nothing, and walked away, going farther up the road. Emille drank the absinthe, limiting herself to only one. She sat for a while until she decided that Luisa had just moved into Emille's past. Then Emille saw an envelope on the floor by the chair where Luisa had sat. She used her foot to pull it within reach and picked it up. The envelope was addressed to Luisa at their apartment, and the return address was an apartment in Bryn Mawr, along with the name of a woman Emille did not recognize. She looked up when she heard Luisa shout her name while running to the café.

"Don't open it!" Luisa came up to the table and grabbed the envelope from Emille. "You didn't read it, did you?" Luisa must have run quite a distance after realizing she had lost her mail. She looked even more intense than she had when she read the letter from her father.

"No, Luisa, I didn't open the envelope. Is there a letter inside? It felt like one. Who is the lady writing to you, and why?"

Luisa slid into a chair and ordered an absinthe from a waitress. Emille nodded that she wanted another one as well. Neither said anything until their drinks were delivered. Luisa raised her glass as a toast, and Emille said, "To art. It's what we are."

Luisa took a page out of the envelope. "This is from my girlfriend back home. It's the real reason I'm going back. I'll make it short. We broke up just before I came to Paris. She didn't approve of my art. And she had another girlfriend. I wrote to her last week and asked if we could get back together. This letter says we can. So that is the real reason I'm going home. I'm sorry to tell you this, but you deserve to know."

Emille sipped her drink, looked firmly at Luisa, and said, "You need a friend like her, not like me. I wish you the best in the world. I really mean that." She put some money on the table and said Luisa should use it to pay for the drinks.

He Quickly Poured a Glass of Wine

The next three days were intense. Jean would get up, paint, eat, paint, eat, paint, and go to bed. That was all he did until he felt the portrait expressed his vision of the couple and their dog. He spent more than an hour just looking at the canvas and then touching it up with a fine brush. He remembered Degas telling others, including him, "One improves a painting at the end with little touches, but when one touch makes it worse, you undo that, and you are done." Jean agreed with that and felt he now could put down the brushes.

As he relaxed, he realized he wanted to have some red wine, perhaps to celebrate the completion of the painting or at least to water down his intense emotions. He changed into something presentable that didn't have paint all over it. He walked to the Café de la Nouvelle Athénes, expecting to spend some time with whichever artists had shown up. Hopefully Emille would be there.

When he got to the café, out of habit, he looked at the spot where his two paintings had hung before the ladies bought them. He could not believe his eyes when he saw a painting of a papillon, clearly Coco and obviously by Emille. He didn't see her at the tables with the other artists. He went up to the painting and stood there for a good while. Eventually, Camille came by and said, "I'll put your pinot noir at the table. The painting is for you. Emille went to Giverny, and Luisa went back to America. Pennsylvania."

Jean felt lost or maybe empty. He stayed at the Coco portrait for a little more time and then went over to the artists' table and took a seat where Camille had put his wine.

"You look dazed, my friend," Degas said. "Do you like your painting? Emille said that it is her gift to you. I'm pleased at how nicely Emille painted. She may have more talent than I gave her credit for. By the way, how is your portrait coming along?"

"Fine, Edgar. I reached the point where a tiny change made it worse, like you said would happen. I did nothing but sleep, paint, eat, paint, eat, paint, and sleep for three-plus days." He quickly poured a glass of wine.

"Jean, Emille asked me to give you this letter," Pissarro said. "We've all read it, so now you will be up to date." Others at the table laughed.

He took the letter and read it to himself.

> Jean, the painting of Coco is for you to have. Luisa has gone to Bryn Mawr. I am in Giverny, taking lessons from Mr. Monet. I am on the outside of the inside versus outside debate since you did the portrait outside. Emille

He looked at Degas. "You lost the debate with her too?"

"No worry. She's not as good as Luisa and may not make it as an artist, although the Papillon is quite good, and I have to admit that. I can take sides now that they have broken up."

Jean wondered if he agreed. From what he had seen of the work by the two, Jean had decided they were different, but neither could be called better than the other. Of course, Jean knew that Degas could paint like the master he was, and he was prone to taking positions just for the purpose of an argument. Jean said nothing in reply.

Fortunately, the conversation turned to the idea of taking sides with students and other artists, and Jean drank his wine while trying to decide what he should do next. He would deliver his painting tomorrow and hang the painting of Coco at his studio. "Edgar, this painting by Emille might actually be better than Luisa could do."

Degas waved his hand at the canvas. "You are right."

Jean quickly drank his wine and then went home.

How Did You Do That?

J ean picked up a second bottle of wine on the way back to his studio and apartment. He needed to sleep, and the wine would help.. Tomorrow he would deliver the portrait; get paid, he assumed; and go to Giverny. Other than sitting at the table for two with Emille, he had no plans. Even garden work would be up to Monet, and he hoped he would be asked to finish the portrait of his son and Blanche.

The next morning, he took a taxi to Charles and Suzanne's lovely home. He went in through the unlocked gate. He put his bag down and handed the painting to Charles, who immediately put it on the easel Jean had used. Charles and Suzanne stood back, came up close, and looked at each other. Charles bent down to look up at the portrait. They didn't say a word, but Charles and Suzanne both made noises of joy. Jean relaxed and then petted Coco.

Charles motioned for Jean to come to the painting. "Our skin looks so real on the painting. How did you do that?"

"In stages. I start with an underpainting, or umber zone. Then I establish the drawing, composition, and so on. After that, I add the local colors to define the big color segments. I add some oil, followed by translucent paint, and adjust the color. Finally, I keep adding translucent layers until my eyes say, 'Enough.'"

"This is wonderful. Suzanne, do you agree?"

"Charles, it's better than wonderful. Even you look great." She laughed and pointed at her husband.

Charles reached into his pocket and counted out the francs to pay Jean. "Here. There's a little more because this painting is more than we expected. You remembered so much."

"Well, thank you. I did make little dabs where I had to be sure of the color. Not really memory, just good technique."

It took Jean half an hour to leave, as both Charles and Suzanne were full of questions and comments. The time with them gave him great compensation for his work. He wanted to stay for more praise but had a train to catch. Finally, the taxi Charles had called honked twice. Charles came out and paid the taxi driver. Jean thanked him, of course, and got into the vehicle with his bag. Suzanne came out to wave, and Coco came out. Jean had the taxi driver wait until they had the dog under control.

He told the driver to take him to the Saint-Lazare station. He had what he needed, including Emille's painting of Coco, and would go directly to Giverny.

Emille and Jean Sat on the Regular Chairs

On the train from Paris, the weather remained nice, but the wind blew smoke into his window, so he closed it and opened the window across the aisle from him. He thought about moving to the other bench, but he could see more farms and haystacks on that side. His thoughts were few and not at all bright. Delivering the portrait had emptied his emotions. Not long after, he fell asleep, as usual.

When Jean reached Giverny, he checked into his room at his apartment. He did not ask where Emille's room was. After unpacking what little he'd brought, he stood at the window, looking at the tree he had painted from that second floor both in perspective and as if he stood on the ground. Good memories warmed him. Then came a knock on his door, which brought him back to the present in his room.

When he opened the door, Blanche and Jean Monet were standing there. As usual, Blanche spoke for them. "Claude wants you to come to dinner soon, and be prepared to talk about our portrait. Emille says you did a wonderful portrait in Paris. Did you get her painting of Coco?"

A door opened and shut down the hall. Emille appeared, holding four wine glasses and a bottle of cabernet sauvignon. "Shall we continue this conversation outside at the little table?" She led the way. Blanche told Jean Monet to get two more chairs. Emille and Jean sat on the regular chairs. The other two's presence did not fit the way he had hoped to be with Emille at the table, but at least she was the one who'd chosen the table.

Emille handed the bottle to him, asking him to open it, which he did. Blanche sat beside Jean, and Jean Monet sat beside Emille, who poured the wine, seemingly oblivious to where people sat. Blanche patted his arm and said, "Welcome back, Jean. Please give us a toast to go with our wine."

He tried briefly to stand up, but Blanche didn't move out of the way. He raised his glass, as did the others. "To art and gardens, both made better by light and color." No one said anything afterward; they just sipped their wine.

Finally, Blanche stood up. "Let's go find your father, Jean. And put these chairs back. Emille, please don't keep him here too long. Claude wants you both to join us for dinner, which will be soon." She bowed to him and then escorted Jean off to find his father.

Emille poured them both more wine. She looked back at the building. "This is a nice place, but I can't live here for much longer. I saw a one-bedroom apartment when we first started looking. Oh heavens, how am I going to live with saying *we*? Luisa and I are no more."

Jean nodded and then wondered if she would say *we* about the two of them. Neither of them spoke for a while, long enough to finish the whole bottle of wine. Finally, he said, "I have dreamed of sitting here with you. But none of my dreams told me what to say."

"Mine either, Jean. Shall we go to dinner? The table will be here later, in case we think of what either of us might say."

This Is Quite Sudden

On his way to dinner, Jean met Alice outside at the green bench, and then he went into the dining room. He took a seat near Monet's son. Blanche came in with her siblings but sat next to Jean. Monet and his wife came in, followed by Emille, who had to sit with the siblings.

Monet pointed to Jean. "You sat next to Blanche, Jean. Why?"

"No, I didn't, Claude. I sat here, and she chose to sit here by me when she came in with her siblings. Besides, what difference does it make?"

Blanche spoke before Monet could respond. "Claude, I sat here because it is the closest chair to your delightful son." She reached around Jean to shake hands with Monet's son. Jean hoped no one noticed how her arm rubbed his shoulder.

"Claude, I meant what I asked," Jean said. "What difference does it make who sits where? Oh, other than you at the head of the table with your wife next to you."

Alice clapped her hands. "We are about to have our first course. Who will say grace? Someone, please."

Blanche stood up, using Jean's shoulder to help her rise. "Let us pray. Loving God, you have gathered us here together to give us a meal together, and we ask your blessing on the food. You have gathered us together as family for fellowship and love. Amen." Her hand held Jean's shoulder—for balance, he hoped—as she sat back down in her chair.

"Thank you, Blanche," Monet said. "Your mother and I appreciate your prayers and thoughts. While we still have a moment, Jean—oh, not my son Jean—will you be able to stay here for a while, perhaps a year or more? I want to build that Japanese bridge at the narrows. You will be in charge. And yes, you will have painting lessons and an opportunity to paint and even go to Paris when you need to. Will you?"

"Claude, my initial reaction is to say yes, I will work with you and improve my abilities as an artist. But this is quite sudden, and I want to think about it for a bit. I'll confirm my decision tomorrow, perhaps when I have this lovely couple sit for their portrait in the morning. When the light is right." He didn't feel comfortable looking down the table at Emille, but he wanted to talk with her—needed to, really—before he committed to Monet. Fortunately, the maid came in with the popular first course: spinach soufflé. It had a wonderful, appetizing aroma.

The maid served Monet first; then the guests; and, finally, Alice. Jean saw the symbolism of including all in their table.

"Jean, my son, you and lovely Blanche will be available for Jean to paint your portrait?" Monet asked. "Good," he added when they both nodded. "My goal for this young artist is to help him become great. He has the talent. Emille, you are not a good artist. Yet. You have the talent to be an excellent artist. Jean, keep her around. Teach her en plein air."

Alice's children were obviously bored with the conversation and started talking among themselves, sometimes including Blanche but not Jean or the other Jean. Dinner went faster then, especially after Alice spoke privately to the maid. After dinner, Emille and Jean agreed to go to the table for two.

Honor Women of Honor

Jean and Emille left Monet's house and walked the path to their apartment building. Jean had walked with Emille alone and with Luisa many times, more than he could remember. They started the walk about two meters apart and slowly came closer to each other. He felt pleased that Emille did some of the getting close. *Should I hold her hand? Put my hand on her shoulder? More?* As he had that debate with himself, his arm slowly swung a bit. Emille took his hand and put it on her shoulder. Then she moved even closer to him. Jean laughed to himself, trying to picture his quizzical smile. *Finally, after wanting a hug for so long, here it is.*

Emille felt uncertain and almost stressed about Jean. She understood she and Jean are not going to have a physical relationship at this time, but she even more intensely wondered if they would ever do that. She wondered what it would be like to go with Jean to Philadelphia to meet her parents and some American artists. Would they take separate ships to preserve her reputation? Maybe her parents would come to France for their wedding. Was what she felt part of what they'd talked about earlier in trying to understand when, if ever, they would get physical?

They came to the courtyard and sat at the table for two. She faced the apartment, and he faced the path. He didn't want company. "So here we are, Emille. Have you thought of something to talk about?"

"Jean, have you?" Her arms were folded a bit tightly.

"Well, you heard what Monet said about my working for him and painting here for a year or more."

"Yes, I heard that. I also heard Monet's concern about you and Blanche. What is that about? And what about me? I don't know that my parents will support me here. Do I go back to Paris? What about me, Jean?"

"Those are a lot of heavy questions. But 'I don't know' is not what I need or want to say." They both were silent for a while. He thought about getting another bottle of red wine from his room but decided he needed to think straight. "Emille, Blanche is just playing games with me to get Jean Monet to show more interest in her. Claude has already decided he wants them to get married."

"That's fine. The family avoids someone new coming in. But, Jean, what about me? Do you want me to go back to Paris? Do you want me to move into your apartment? Do you expect me to sleep with you? Tell me."

Jean almost wished someone would come along and want to sit

with them, but he knew he had to talk straight to her. "Emille, I am not a virgin. I don't know any French man who is, at least over age twenty. Does that surprise you? It shouldn't. There are many women in Paris. Look at who you see in Montmartre. But there are moral men, like myself, who honor women of honor. You are a woman of honor. So maybe men take a different approach with those other women, like Camille, though I have not touched and will not touch her."

"Camille doesn't matter. You have talked about yourself. Your work and painting. Your honor. You have not said one word answering my question. What about me? Good night, Jean. I will see you at breakfast."

Emille stood up to go into the building but stopped when Monet called out to her.

"Emille, please wait a moment! I would like to talk to both of you." He went to get an extra chair, and Emille returned to hers. "Emille, I hope I didn't offend you at dinner when I said you are not a good artist. I did say that you could be good. Very good. That's why I told Jean to teach you en plein air painting. He is still learning, but he is already very good."

"He may be a good artist, Mr. Monet, but right now, he's all about himself. I begged him to answer my question 'What about me?' and he just talked about himself."

"Is that true, Jean?" Monet leaned on the little table, coming closer to him. "What is it? Won't she sleep with you? Do you have someone else?"

"No, Claude. None of that stuff. Like I said at dinner, yours is an overwhelming offer, and I need to understand what it means in my life. As far as Emille in my life, she and I have talked about it but come to no conclusions yet." Jean turned to face Emille. "I'm sorry, Emille. You didn't deserve for me not to answer you. The problem is, I don't have an answer. I want you to be part of my life. I do. And I want to do it with honor."

Monet laughed and got out of his chair. "That sounds like a proposal to me, Emille. Are you going to say yes?"

She just looked at Monet. Jean looked at her. When she looked at him, their eyes locked. She smiled, picked up her empty wine glass, offered a toast, and said, "Yes."

Monet looked back at Jean. "Jean, can you find a way to get married?"

"In Pennsylvania!" Emille said, her hands on her hips.

"Jean, my offer is still open for at least a year of work and free lessons. Can you get married in Philadelphia on an afternoon soon and come back here to work and paint? You'll have your honeymoon on the ship."

Afterword

Claude Monet and his family stayed at his house in Giverny. Blanche and Jean Monet were married, as he wished. Sadly, his wife, Alice, died in 1911. Blanche cared for Monet for the rest of his life, including through cataracts and other health concerns. His favorite child, Jean, died in 1914. Monet died on December 5, 1926, and is buried in the Giverny church cemetery.

In 1966, Claude Monet's heirs donated the property and art to the French Academy of Fine Arts. The property was restored and opened to the public in 1980.

Jean and Emille are fictional characters, so their future can be imagined.

Bibliography

The following sources were invaluable to me in researching *Light and Color: Inside or Outside*. I also found valuable information on the internet, such as recipes for lunch and dinner.

Bordman, Aileen, and Derek Fell. *Monet's Palate Cookbook*. Gibbs Smith, 2015, Layton, Utah.

Hériteau, Jaqueline, and Charles B. Thomas. *Water Gardens*. Boston: Houghton Mifflin Company, 1994.

Murray, Elizabeth. *Photographs for Monet's Passion: The Gardens at Giverny, 2014 Engagement Calendar*. Portland, Oregon: Pomegranat Communications, 2014.

Murray, Elizabeth. *Photographs for Monet's Passion: The Gardens at Giverny, 2016 Engagement Calendar*. Portland, Oregon: Pomegranat Communications, 2016.

Orr, Lynn Federle, Paul Hayes Tucker, and Elizabeth Murray. *Monet: Late Paintings of Giverny from the Musée Marmottan*. San Francisco: Fine Arts Museum of San Francisco, 1994.

Roe, Sue. *In Montmartre: Picasso, Matisse and the Birth of Modernist Art*. New York: Penguin Press, 2014.

Roe, Sue. *The Private Lives of the Impressionists*. New York: Harper Perennial, 2007.

Stuckey, Charles F. *Claude Monet 1840–1926*. Chicago: Art Institute of Chicago; New York: Thames and Hudson, 1995.

Tucker, Paul Hayes. *Monet: In the 20th Century*. New Haven: Yale University Press, 1998.

Wildenstein, Daniel. *Monet's Years at Giverny: Beyond Impressionism*. New York: Metropolitan Museum of Art, 1978.

Printed in the United States
By Bookmasters